Dad, in Spirit

Dad, in Spirit

A. LaFaye

Simon & Schuster Books for Young Readers
New York London Toronto Sydney Singapore

SIMON & SCHUSTER BOOKS FOR YOUNG READERS
An imprint of Simon & Schuster Children's Publishing Division
1230 Avenue of the Americas, New York, New York 10020
Text copyright © 2001 by Alexandria LaFaye
SIMON & SCHUSTER BOOKS FOR YOUNG READERS
is a trademark of Simon & Schuster.
Book design by Paul Zakris
The text of this book is set in 13-point Berkeley Oldstyle.
Printed in the United States of America
10 9 8 7 6 5 4 3 2 1

Library of Congress Cataloging-in-Publication Data
LaFaye, A.
Dad, in spirit / A. LaFaye.
p. cm.
Summary: Ebon's father, who is in a coma, appears to the family
as a wandering spirit, and Ebon must reunite the spirit and
the body before it is too late.
ISBN 0-689-81514-X
[1. Astral projection—Fiction.] I. Title
PZ7.L1413 Dad 2001
[Fic]—dc21
00-052224

Thank you, David, John, and Michael, for your patience, hard work, and perseverance. You helped me remold this book into its present form. I also appreciate all the hard work of the people "behind the scenes" at Simon & Schuster. I'd also like to thank George Nicholson for getting me started in this wonderful business. Nancy Willard, a magical woman of wit, wisdom, and kindness, gave me great advice and support in the early stages of this book. Thank you, Nancy. I shall be eternally grateful to God for the opportunity to be a writer and the chance to share my stories with others.

To Patrick Paul LaFaye—the man who could become Jerry Lewis, Clem Kaddiddlehopper, Stan Laurel, and Tommy Smothers at will. I'm so grateful for all of the laughter and the love. Thanks for growing up with me and never letting go of the child inside. I love you, Dad.

CONTENTS

DAD, IN SPIRIT

Halloween, Jones Style

Jack-o'-lanterns lit up our front lawn like supernatural yard lights. The dust-spitting whine of Mom's stone grinder buzzed through the dark around them as she scrambled to fill all her gargoyle orders. After working a full day down at the Guardian Insurance office, she chiseled away on miscarved tombstones to make those spooky stone dudes. She usually made a few of them for craft fairs and such, but come fall the orders poured in like fan mail.

My older sister, Joliet, had gone into full production mode too. A few years ago she sewed the costumes for the sixth-grade production of *Peter Pan*. Marisa Ortiz liked her Peter costume so much she wore it for Halloween that year. Pretty soon all the kids in school wanted a Joliet Jones original for trick-or-treating. To keep up with the demand, Joliet would start working on new designs in January. She'd get enough orders for costumes to keep her sewing almost every night from the beginning of school to Halloween—she had the stereo, the new clothes, and the college fund to prove it. That girl made enough money to stake a high roller at an Atlantic City craps table. Dad even had to build a sewing annex onto her room so she could store all the costumes. That place filled up, rack by rack, with fairies, grim reapers, courtiers, griffins, and swans waiting to come to life.

Last year she transformed my suit-wearing principal, Mrs. Gilford, into a fairy godmother—sparkly dress, corset, wand, and all. I couldn't wait to see what Joliet turned her into next.

Meanwhile, my little brother, Samuel, wandered through the house memorizing every ghost story ever presented as the truth. He wanted to know them all—from the phantom handprint left by a window-cleaning fireman who died in the fire that called him away from his housekeeping duties, to the wispy flapper who haunted the site of the Chicago dance hall where she died, sighted by dancers, passersby, and cabbies alike.

My favorite one was about the relative who refused to leave. Uncle Otto continued to rock away the night hours in his bedroom years after he died. When the family talked about selling the house, Otto cast his vote by taking his bedroom door off the hinges and throwing it down the stairs. That little temper tantrum clinched it for the family. They moved out in a jiffy.

Dad kept busy haunting the local Y. As a carpenter who treated each new project like an invention, he took on the job of annual curator for our neighborhood haunted house. The Y built a new place a few years back and made plans to tear down the old Victorian building, but Dad wouldn't hear of it. He promised he'd keep the Y in clean towels if they'd let him turn the old place into a haunted house every year. He did more than keep his promise. Last year they made enough money to add a whirlpool.

Dad didn't go for ghouly sound tracks, strobe lighting, grape eyeballs, or spaghetti guts. He actually converted the old Y building into a moaning, creaky spook house complete with secret passages, projected spirits, and floating objects. Folks came from as far as Wisconsin to see Dad's yearly spectacle in our small neighborhood here in Minneapolis.

With the rest of the family in full festival mode, that left me, Ebon Jones, the boring member of the Jones Family Halloween Quintet. I'd never wind up on the Oscar stage accepting an award for costume design like Joliet. I couldn't give a whole audience a coat of goose bumps the way Samuel did every time he told a ghost story. Even with Dad's help, my Boy Scout birdhouse had looked like it'd been built on a hill in a strong wind. And the one time I tried to carve something out of rock, I ended up chipping a hole right through Mom's workbench. Nope, I was just plain old Ebon Jones. I spent my time helping out where I could—hunting down new tales for Samuel, polishing stone ghoulies for Mom, basting for Joliet, or fetching tools for Dad.

Gopher duties aside, I guess I had one talent. I could solve a mean puzzle. Weird as it sounds, I actually loved doing word problems on math tests. Give me a puzzle and I was in mental heaven. I loved how you could twist and turn things around in your head until they became new things. I guess Dad was the same way. That was why he loved remodeling Hamilton Hall year after year—it was a puzzle he had to take apart and put back together again.

I would've loved to do more than just fetch tools for Dad while he remodeled Hamilton Hall, but he was a solo show. He didn't even let me help when he was researching. Haunting historical societies, libraries, and any reference database available online, Dad did background research for authors. If they wanted to do a book set at a Maine hotel that burned down a hundred years ago, Dad would find out what kind of towels hung in the bathroom, if he could. And when his brain was in danger of bursting if he didn't tell someone about all the cool facts he'd learned, he hunted me down. He'd wake me up in the middle of the night to tell me about his newest discovery. Take Charles Goodyear as an example. Dad found out that the first few times the guy thought he'd invented vulcanized rubber (that's rubber that doesn't easily melt), he sold rubber coats, shirts, and underwear. You'd think the guy had invented the button, the way people snatched up his clothes. Too bad they couldn't keep them once they'd put them on on a hot summer day. They melted. Can you imagine walking down the street and having your underwear melt down your leg? That's what you get for buying rubber drawers in the first place, I guess.

Yeah, the stories Dad shared were really cool, but I

would've loved to be more than his audience or his gopher. See, no one but Dad was allowed inside the Hamilton Hall Haunted House until Halloween night. He was always squawking over the walkie-talkie to get me to run over with some gadget or another, then meeting me at a back door.

Dad always unveiled his newest incarnation of Hamilton Hall on Halloween, but he insisted on having everything done so he could take the day before Halloween off. He usually needed the rest. Hamilton Hall was open only one night, so people started coming as soon as it got dark, and kept filing through until dawn. The line went all the way to the end of the block throughout the night.

Two days before Halloween was Dad's last chance for finishing everything, so he'd started working at dawn. As his designated gopher, I'd made enough runs to and from Hamilton Hall to wear a new path through our back woods. At half past eight I heard Dad shout, "Well, nail me in a coffin till morning, I'm done!"

Grabbing up the walkie-talkie, I shouted to congratulate Dad as I ran downstairs. Dad sang "Celebration" at full blast as I darted through Samuel's room, down the back stairs to Joliet's room, then down the front stairs and through the kitchen to Mom's workshop.

Stopping at the front door, I met Dad as he walked in, still singing.

"Are we ready?" he shouted up the stairs. Tall enough to touch the bottom of the chandelier in our ten-foot-high front hall, Dad was a big guy with a lot of lung room, so you could hear him all the way up to the fourth floor, where I hung out.

Everyone showed up in a flash, ready to celebrate. The Jones family always celebrated at Kingston's, the restaurant where you ordered dessert first. We'd start with a caramel chocolate pie, then launch into a garbage pizza—everything on it from pepperoni to tuna. We'd eat the toppings with a fork, then roll up the crust like a burrito and dip it in pizza sauce. It was the best.

Dad made sure we got one of their private rooms so we could have our own celebration. We'd downed dessert before Joliet even finished telling us about the dragon costume she had just finished for the Tinsdale triplets.

We cheered the waiter when he brought the pizza. Harpooning Joliet's discarded pepperonis with a toothpick, I leaned over to ask Dad, "Could you help me study for my math test?"

I could do a word problem with half my brain in reverse, but long division and decimal points tied my thoughts into knots. And there was no way I'd ask my little brother for help. Samuel did math problems in his sleep. I'd heard him mumbling his way through the multiplication tables when he snoozed during car trips. Thanks to him, I was the only fourth grader with a younger brother in his class.

Dipping pizza crust into his milk, Dad said, "Sure, sure. When we get home."

Dad said "sure" like most people answer the greeting "Hi, how you doing?" People just say, "I'm good. What's up with you?" even when they've just flunked a math test. Dad didn't mean that he'd study with me. Maybe he meant it in the way people who want to let you know they care about you do when they ask how you're doing, but they really don't want to know the details—they've got better things to do. Dad probably wanted to help me study, but knowing him, he'd get drawn into a late-night research project and forget all about it.

Turning to Samuel, Dad said, "How about a dry run on your show for tomorrow night?"

"Okay."

Mom turned down the lights so we could all listen to Samuel tell tales of the dead returning to the land of the living. He had to practice for the big night. As the pretour entertainment at Hamilton Hall, he stood out front on a black-veiled stage murmuring his stories into a microphone, while Mom ran the sound board, Joliet outfitted the ghoulies who ran around inside, and Dad played the part of special effects wizard. Me, I collected tickets.

As Samuel led us down a dark, winding road in Hudson, Wisconsin, to investigate an eerie glow under a bridge on Cooley Road, Mom said, "Luke Jones, what is this on your head?"

"Nothing," Dad insisted.

"Joliet, get the lights," Mom said.

Joliet jumped up and fumbled for the switch.

As the light came on, Mom stood up to inspect the back of Dad's head. "There's a welt back here large enough to be harboring a golf ball."

"It's a hazard of the trade. I took a little spill. That's all." Dad took off the old conductor's cap he always wore while constructing, and rubbed his head.

"You could have a concussion."

Dad turned to her, his eyes crossed, "Why, are my pupils dilated?"

"Cut it out." Mom swatted him.

"It only hurts when I blink." Dad fluttered his eyes.

"One of these years you're going to fall and impale yourself on a screwdriver. Nobody will find you for days, and all the visitors will think you're one of the attractions."

"Now, that'd be a showstopper." Dad nodded.

Mom shook her head, knowing there was no stopping Dad. Safety ruined the fun in his mind. He had scrapes, scars, bumps, and memories of broken bones as evidence of all the fun he'd had in his life.

After Kingston's we went to Bailey's Lawn Ornaments and Monuments. We had a blast. Mom wandered around with her flashlight getting ideas. The rest of us played hide-and-seek. It was more like hide-and-find with us. Dad always found everyone.

He loved being it. He'd count to two hundred so everyone could find a real good hiding place, then "sneak find" us all. He'd shout, "Here I come! Hide your toes!" Then he'd fall silent. He didn't talk. He didn't shuffle his feet. I never even heard him breathe. You couldn't tell the hunt had begun.

One minute I'd be peeking around the hairy arm of the stone gorilla I'd hidden behind, then Dad'd be leaning over the gorilla's shoulder, saying, "Do you think he eats stone bananas?"

It never failed—Dad would count, we would hide, then he'd show up out of nowhere to strike up a conversation. We never let *him* hide because we couldn't find him! We preferred to get mad at him for sneaking up on us and chase him until we couldn't breathe.

We'd tackle Dad, then tickle him. His laugh sounded so much like those little rubber drums that squeak when you shake them. He turned such a bright red, you'd think he'd been dropped into a vat of cherry Kool-Aid. He looked so funny we'd start laughing and fall over. We'd all end up in a giggling, gasping heap on the ground.

That night Samuel started the chase. He had found this great hiding place wedged between two stacks of huge concrete blocks. Hiding across from him beneath a giant mushroom, I saw Dad crawling over the top block.

He moved so quick and smooth, for a second I thought he could be one of those catlike superheroes (Catman or Pumar), moving through the night without a sound, pouncing on his victims. Then Dad slid down into the crack headfirst like a snake. His beat-up old train conductor's hat fell on Samuel's shoulder as Dad said, "Howdy. I'm looking for the ceramic squirrels. Seen any?"

"Dad!" Samuel screamed, reaching up to grab him. "I hate it when you do that!"

Dad pulled himself back up to the top of the pile, saying, "It's the object of the game, Samuel. Would you prefer that I cheated?"

Samuel came out of the bottom row of his hiding place just as Dad jumped to the ground. He lunged at Dad. "You do cheat!"

Dad jumped backward, laughing. "Do I?"

"I'll get you!" Samuel shouted, and the chase was on. Dad started to run, Samuel pursued him. I ran too.

Samuel chased Dad toward the open field beyond the uncarved headstones. I put on the steam to catch up. Joliet almost flattened me when she jumped down off a stack of concrete flower boxes. We collided and teetered, laughing as we got under way again. Dad had already reached the field. He was so tall, it was like he had seven-league boots! He could cover practically a quarter of an acre in a couple of strides.

Dad turned, then started to jog from left to right so we could catch up. Samuel dived at Dad's legs, hitting him in the knees. Dad crumbled to the ground. As usual, Joliet came to Dad's rescue and tackled Samuel. Those two laughed as I jumped in and went for Dad. He hadn't moved. He just lay there. He'd been known to play dead, but I felt this time was different (of course, I always did, and he got me every time).

I dropped down beside him, shouting, "Dad!" His eyes closed, his head turned to the side, he looked as if he'd fallen asleep.

"Cut it out, Dad." I shoved him.

The others had stopped goofing off. They stood over Dad, staring down at him as if his head had gone missing—all big eyed and openmouthed.

"Come on, Dad. Joke's up!" I pinched his cheek.

"Mom's coming!" Joliet screamed.

I turned. Mom ran at full bore, her fuchsia scarf floating along behind her. Seeing Mom made everybody panic. If she came running, Dad must be in trouble. Just then, Dad flew up in the air as if he'd been jolted with electricity.

Blinking, he realized he was surrounded and started to yell and tickle anyone within arm's reach. When Mom showed up, tickling fingers ready, and laughing, we all figured it was a joke and joined in the ticklefest.

I laughed so hard my ribs hurt on the way home. The whole night turned out to be one great Jones family adventure. I went to bed happy as a dragon with a cave full of treasure.

Dad?

The next morning started out pretty normal in a bran-muffin kind of way. I ate Kookleberry Captain Crackle for breakfast. I flicked the kookleberries at Samuel. I hated those pukey little balls, and he was a good target. He always listened to his headphones at breakfast. That morning he recited math problems—312 divided by 3 equals 104; 246 divided by 12 equals 20.5. He'd probably recorded a portion of his math book to memorize for our test that day. What a twerp.

I could solve any word problem you plopped down in front of me, but a lot of math was just stupid numbers. I'd probably fail that dumb test, no thanks to Dad. He'd promised to help me study, but he'd forgotten all about it by the time we got home. Big surprise. Dad could remember the days of the week each president got married, but he couldn't remember when he'd made a promise to do something with me. I hated depending on Dad to keep his promises. Instead of working through problems with a guy who could make a game out of learning the periodic table of elements, I had to listen to Samuel spouting off the last two chapters of our text-book. Both of them deserved to be pelted with kookleberries. And since Dad still hadn't gotten up yet, I let Samuel have it.

Some people can't chew gum and walk at the same time, but Samuel wasn't capable of listening to his headphones and keeping his eyes open. In my way of thinking, when his brain went into overdrive, his body went into reverse.

I guess it was cool, in a way. I could hit him right between the eyes with a kookleberry (most kids could dodge me). *Pow!* His eyes snapped open as the pink milk oozed down his nose.

"Mom!" he screamed.

Mom didn't look up from the newspaper as she said, "Ebon, you jettison one more piece of cereal and you're mopping the kitchen floor."

Samuel stuck his tongue out. It was purple as usual. That kid was addicted to grape juice.

"You're such a creep, Ebon," Joliet moaned.

I didn't think about Dad until the two-minute alarm on the stove went off. Dad slept in a lot because he stayed up so late hunting down oddball historical facts on the Internet for his authors. But he never missed saying good-bye.

Sometimes he showed up at the bottom of the stairs wearing his flying-toaster housecoat and basset hound slippers, or he shouted from his closet window. I didn't see him shuffling down the stairs with his hair looking like the victim of a static storm when I went to get my coat from the closet under the stairs.

I didn't really worry until we got outside. Joliet already sat in the car—goofy dads were worse than dorky little brothers on school days as far as she was concerned. Samuel messed around with his raincoat. He loved the way it crinkled when he moved, so he pretended to do a walk on the moon or something. I jumped off the front steps, then turned to wave at Dad. He wasn't there.

Joliet says I wear my heart in my pocket. I felt like it fell right in there when I saw that empty window. It was almost like Dad was my twin brother instead of my father. I could tell when he was in trouble. I ran back inside, nearly knocking Samuel over as he planted a pretend flag. I'd climbed the stairs before Mom could shout, "Last one out the door jogs behind the car!"

Dad slept on his stomach, his arm tucked under his chest, one foot sticking out over the edge of the bed.

"Dad?" I knelt down and gave him a little shove. He didn't even moan.

I can't tell the rest. I get all shivery inside when I think of the ambulance, those strange people in white poking Dad with all those needles and tubes, the crackly radio, and screaming sirens. It all happened in slow motion. I watched from the hallway, seeing Dad lying on his back, those people in white hovering over him like anonymous angels looking for the reason Dad wouldn't wake up. Mom sat next to the pillow stroking Dad's hair, saying, "Luke? Luke?" She kept repeating his name as if he were just too tired to answer. I wanted to scream. I wanted to yell so loud the lightbulbs in the fixture above would break into a zillion pieces, "DAD, WAKE UP!"

He didn't.

Coma

We sat in the hospital waiting room like three kids called to the principal's office—silent, scared, and shaking. I swam around in my head fishing for a way to put my heart back where it belonged and stop shivering. I couldn't even keep the images in my mind from shaking loose. One minute I saw Dad smiling at me over the shoulder of a stone gorilla. A second later Dad lay facedown on his pillow.

I wished B. J. were sitting next to me. My best friend and the greatest person to have around when your mind was falling into pieces, B. J. could keep calm during Armageddon. Her dad had a blizzard-size fit over things as little as leaving the cap off the toothpaste. Thanks to him, she'd learned to be calm during any kind of storm.

I could have used a couple pounds of her calmness, but I didn't want to leave the spot where Mom told us to wait. I tried to think of Dad working on secret panels in Hamilton Hall, but then Joliet popped out of her seat like someone had poked her with a pin. "I'm going to find Mom."

Joliet walked off. I watched her go down the long white hallway, with its school-tile floor, then through a window-less metal door.

Watching the clock overhead tick made me tired. I started to think about how much Dad loved to sleep. If he wasn't building or hunting down the origins of the flush toilet, traveling to remote county historical societies, playing with us kids in Castle Rook (the castle he built in our backyard) or acting out books with Mom, Dad's favorite thing to do was dream. He even ate cucumbers before going to sleep because some Dr. Dodo-ologist said it gave you wackier dreams. Mom said all it did was make Dad burp in his sleep.

Dad falling asleep in a permanent kind of way had to be ironic or something. I used to think irony meant food that tastes like iron, the way it does when you have strep throat, but Dad told me it meant you expect one thing and get another. The thing you get is either too much or the exact opposite of the thing you wanted. Dad loved to sleep, and now he was asleep for good. That was ironic.

I took a deep breath to keep from crying. I told myself Dad would wake up if I didn't give in. Crying meant I didn't believe he'd leave the hospital with us and take us out for hot-fudge sundaes at Sebastian Joe's. I wanted him to be the one to walk through the door at the end of the hall, but Joliet did.

"She's on the phone with her boss," Joliet said as she sat down.

Samuel whispered, "Why can't we be with Dad?"

"Read the sign." I pointed to the door. Screwed to the

wall at adult height, the sign read, NO CHILDREN UNDER 16 YEARS OF AGE ALLOWED BEYOND THIS POINT. If they weren't going to let us in to be with our mom and dad, the least they could have done was put the sign lower—say it to our face.

"Oh." Samuel sighed. "How long do we have to wait?"

"Long enough," Joliet answered.

I hated it when she turned mean. What did Samuel do? He was just scared like me. I kept lying to myself though. If I didn't think bad thoughts, Dad would be okay.

Samuel and Joliet started a fight, but I didn't listen. I just sat there trying to list off the U.S. presidents in order, to keep my mind off Dad. . . . George Washington, John Adams, Thomas Jefferson and . . . the M. & M. guys I never remember . . . and . . . John blah-blah Adams . . . Mom showed up before I could think of his middle name.

"No news yet, troops." Mom sat down on the couch, and just like we did when it was time to pop in a movie, all three of us kids piled in around her, Samuel on her lap, Joliet and I on either side of her. Dad rarely watched with us. He said movies had to be the biggest waste of valuable researching time. Mom saw our movie nights as good cuddle time. Closing my eyes, I could almost imagine us back into the TV room.

"I can't stand the waiting," Joliet said.

"Then how about a prayer?" Mom gave Joliet a squeeze. "Dad could use God in his corner right now."

"That never works," I said, remembering how hard I'd prayed to get a mountain bike for Christmas.

Mom tweaked my ear. "Hey, God's not a mail-order catalog." She knew exactly what I meant. I'd told her how my pray-for-a-bike campaign had failed.

"Don't forget Barron," Samuel said.

Joliet moaned. "Not again."

"I like this story." Mom smiled.

"When Uncle Todd turned ten, they found out that his dog, Gin, had cancer." Samuel had taken on the role of family historian a few years back and always supplied a family tale on cue. "Uncle Todd prayed and prayed that God would heal his dog, but they had to put Gin to sleep."

I figured I could hurry things along a bit, so I said, "And Uncle Todd said he didn't believe in God anymore."

Mom said, "Let him finish."

"Grandma Winslow told him God always answers our prayers with what we need, not what we want. And two weeks after Gin died, a new puppy showed up out of the cornfield. Uncle Todd knew as soon as that little guy licked his face—God had answered his prayer. And they named him Barron."

"How sweet." Joliet rolled her eyes. That started a shoving match.

"Truce." Mom shouldered her way between them. "If you ask me, Dad's not the only who needs a little help through this. If you're not going to pray, just sit for a while. Relax."

I kept my prayer simple. "God, please send Dad back to us."

After the amen I sat there thinking it didn't seem right to compare Dad's situation to the life of two dogs. And the whole putting-to-sleep part gave me the chills. Dad had to be okay. I didn't just *want* that to happen. I *needed* it. I missed Dad enough already.

Sometimes Dad's office became a black hole. He'd get sucked into some research project and not come out for days except to fill his plate or hit the john. Dad found out all kinds of cool things, like the fact that Abraham Lincoln kept all of his important papers in his hat, but crazy facts didn't make up for all the softball games, piano recitals, and plays Dad missed out on. Dad promised to show up, but those promises dissolved when a new fact-finding mission pulled him in. And now he'd been pulled into a black hole of sleep. Would he ever come out?

If anyone but God knew the answer to that question, it should've been Dad's doctor. She showed up just after Mom said, "Amen."

This doctor didn't wear one of those eye-hurting white coats. Instead, she wore a jogging suit. One of those shushy nylon things that makes all the noise when you walk. As the doctor approached, Mom pulled us closer.

"Mrs. Jones." She nodded to Mom, then sat down on the floor and folded her legs up in front of her, saying, "Kids, I'm Dr. Parker."

I wanted to say, "We know that." We'd met when she set Dad's leg after he fell off the roof of Castle Rook during the final stages of building. Did she think we didn't remember that whole fiasco?

"I wanted to talk to you about your dad."

"Is he dead?" Joliet asked, her face wet and red from crying.

Joliet's question knocked the wind out of me. I gasped for a breath as Dr. Parker smiled and squeezed Joliet's hand. "No, sweetheart."

My lungs expanded again.

"What's wrong with him?" Samuel almost fell off Mom's lap.

I wanted to put my hand over his mouth to keep him quiet so Dr. Parker could tell us, but Joliet did it for me.

"It's okay, Joliet." Mom patted her knee, but Joliet pushed her hand away.

Dr. Parker tried to tell us how the body can fall asleep so hard it can't feel, hear, see, taste, or smell anything, but I wanted to know why. Why would Dad go into a coma?

B. J.'s grandfather was diabetic, and he went into a coma because he didn't have enough sugar in his blood. Dad ate candy like a chimp eats bananas. His veins were sugarcoated. There had to be another reason for Dad's big sleep.

Dr. Parker said they'd be giving Dad all sorts of tests to find the reason. She told us the first test would be a CAT scan. Samuel giggled. He laughs at the most serious things. A CAT scan meant they were going to shoot X rays into Dad's head so they could see thin layers of the stuff his body was made of instead of just his bones.

Dad had explained it all to me when he did research for a book about a guy with a brain tumor so small the doctors couldn't find it even with a CAT scan. Maybe that was the problem—Dad had a brain tumor. But brain tumors gave you headaches and made your vision go blurry for a long time before you went into a coma. Dad didn't have those problems. No, it couldn't be that, but he did hit his head. First when he fell in Hamilton Hall, then again when Samuel knocked him over. It was Samuel's fault.

I shouted, "He hit his head!"

Everybody stared at me like I'd just announced I was about to explode, then Dr. Parker said, "Yes, Ebon. We were able to determine that your dad has a minor concussion, but that injury wasn't severe enough to cause a coma."

"What now?" Joliet asked.

"Now we try to determine what is causing the coma and wait for your dad to wake up."

Wait? I couldn't wait.

Research

Dr. Parker tried to send us home, saying there was nothing more we could do. I think they learn that line in medical school. All the doctors on TV say it, but it isn't true. I could find out why Dad went into a coma. There had to be a reason. No one else seemed to care, but I did. I was going to find the cause of Dad's coma and reverse it.

I lay in bed that night trying to find a reason for Dad's long sleep, but I kept hearing my mother ask, "You all right, Luke?" I could see Dad fall, his head crashing against a rock.

Counting didn't clear my mind. Humming didn't either, so I started to pace the room. Everything I did just made the images in my mind clearer and Mom's voice louder. I shook on the inside, my skin felt cold. My body started to go out of control, then my mind wandered off, noticing how dark the house had become.

The darkness made me think of Dad's nightly habits. The house was never entirely dark when Dad worked. He'd get up in the middle of the night to hop on the computer. He liked to do research on the Internet after midnight—less traffic. Before he went to his study, he'd do his nightly rounds, turning on the hall lights as he went. Our house was pretty huge (big enough to get lost in, B. J. said) but it echoed, so I could hear Dad when he was on the ground floor even though my bedroom was on the fourth floor. Here's a map of the house, so you can see what I mean:

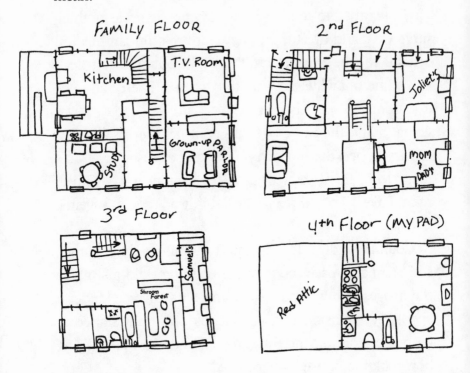

Sometimes I'd hear him roaming the halls, going from bedroom to bedroom to make sure everyone had fallen asleep. If he started to feel lonely, he'd make another round through the house. Part of him was glad to put covers over us when we kicked them off or to pick a teddy bear up off the floor. I know because I'd pretended to be asleep when I wasn't, just so I could see what it felt like to have him cover me up and retrieve Wendell, my stuffed alligator, then give me a kiss on the forehead. Call me Mr. Mushy, but it felt like he'd given me a great, big, juiced-up hug after I'd been away at camp for a week—all warmth and love.

What made Dad even happier was if someone hadn't fallen asleep yet. He'd plop down on the floor and say, "Guess what I found?" Learning new things always made him go goofy. He couldn't wait for breakfast.

I remember when he researched a book on castles years ago. I've got a movie of it in my head. He woke me up one night. Didn't even bother to check and see if I was awake. He shook me until I listened.

"Did you ever think about living in a castle?" he asked.

"Dad, it's the middle of the night!"

"No it's not." Dad tapped the window shade next to my bed (well, he could reach more than three feet, so it was really a ways away). "There's sunshine out there, my boy."

I peeked. A pink purple glow shone through the sliver of glass showing at the bottom of my window.

"It's not dawn yet." I buried my head in the pillow.

"Don't get technical." He shook me. "Come on, Ebon. I want to share this stuff."

"Tell Mom."

"She's making creatures of the night."

That was what Dad called Mom's gargoyles. She'd just

started back then, and she carved them all the time. We had tons of them in our kitchen. They were like a creepy gray mold we couldn't get rid of.

"Okay." I sat up.

Dad smiled, saying, "How'd you like to sleep in a bedroom as big as this one when it's below zero outside if our house had stone walls, no glass in the windows, only wood shutters, and a fireplace as far away as your sink over there?" Dad had a way of speaking in extremely long sentences that made you think he'd run out of breath and faint before he got to the end.

I got the chills just thinking about the castle bedroom. My bedroom was totally cool. I had my own kitchen and bathroom—a regular pad. But it wouldn't be if it was made of stone and butt-freezing cold. "Good thing there are no castles in Minnesota."

"Ha-ha," Dad said, getting up. He squirmed into my bed. Resting his ankles on the baseboard, he put his arm around me and kept talking. For an hour he told me everything about castles, from how the people who lived there got water to where they went to the bathroom. I even learned they put hay on the floor to soak up the food they dropped and the poop from the animals they kept inside. Can you imagine having a pig running around your house?

Everything he said fascinated me. I went to school too tired to think about anything but castles. I even wrote a paper on it and got an A. Here it is:

Ebon Jones
Mrs. Tinker's Class
Social Studies – Extra Credit
Spring Term

A

"A Time of Castles and Kings"

by Ebon Jones

England wasn't always just one big country with a president and a queen to run the county. Along time again in another century England was a bunch of little countries called fifes and Each fife had it's own kind who lived in a castle. All the kings wanted to have a big fight. The bigger the fife the more money they made from the crops they're servants (called serfs) grew. So Kings fought each other to take over fifes. You know like Kind Arthur and the Knights of the Round Table Lancelot and Galahad and those guys. They all fought to make Arthur's kingdom bigger. In war, kings needed castles to keep them safe. They had big stone walls around them so no one could get in and lots of towers so the knights could go up there and look out the windows to see if anybody was coming. And it's really hard to shoot through stone walls when you only have crossbows. They also had a moat. It's kind of a ditch around the castle that the serfs dug up and filled with water and maybe crocodiles so the attacking guys couldn't get over it to the castle. Guns weren't invented yet. Kings didn't always lead armies to attack other castles and collect crops from serfs. Sometimes they had parties. Kings were Christian. They believed in God and saints. Saints are really special people who help others do well. They are so nice they get to sit next to God in Heaven and are called saints. (My Dad says Mother Theresa should be a saint for all the good she does for people.). The days those saints were born, did something special, or died where holidays like St. Patrick's Day. He's a saint cause he got all the rats out of Ireland. Dad says that's the Pied Piper (Sorry). St. Patrick brought Christianity to Ireland. Anyway, his Saint's day is March 17. A king would invite all of his serfs and knights to have a party to honor St. Patrick that day. I learned all this stuff from talking with my Dad. He does research for authors writing books about knights and people like that. What Dad didn't tell me, I looked up in the library's books on knights.

prime minister

King

fife?

their

how about putting this up with your discussion of crossbows?

You certainly know a lot about saints & their holidays!

Your dad's right.

Interesting report, Ebon!

Not all of Dad's groovy facts made it into my paper, but I was so proud of myself for coming up with cool questions like, how'd they make the blocks square? And where did the knights sleep when they weren't fighting for the king? But by the time I got home from school, Dad had started to build one. Typical.

A year before, Joliet had brought home a project on the Old West. She'd been asked to make a diorama of a town called Dogwood from the olden days in the West, so Dad took her straight to the library. They looked at book after book on the Old West (or so Joliet said). Anyway, a week later Dad announced at dinner that he'd be building a new Old West playground at school if the local Lion's Club got the funding. After a great chili cook-off fund-raiser, Dad hit the playground. His Dogwood playground was up and running by the next fall. He was unstoppable.

Dad always did things no other dad would even think of doing—building castles, eating cucumbers before bed, and waking me up in the middle of the night. The night he fell asleep, I got up to go to the bathroom and wondered what Dad was up to.

I didn't go down to see what he was doing, because I wanted to stay mad at him for not helping me study. If I marched into his office to tell him how I felt, he'd pull me into whatever fact hunt he'd started, then we'd talk until dawn about something that wasn't even slightly related to math. I'd probably fall asleep during my math test. And it'd all be a repeat performance of the last time I tried to talk to Dad at night.

If I *had* gone downstairs, I would've known Dad hadn't

gotten up to do research. I'd have gone into his room, and maybe he would've just been sleeping then. I could've woken him up. He'd have gone to the doctor. She would've fixed whatever was wrong, and I could've gone to school and taken my math test.

But no. I didn't go downstairs and Dad didn't wake up. I thought about it for a while, then I wondered, *Well, what was Mom doing? Why didn't she wake him up? How could she not notice that he was in a coma beside her?*

I ran downstairs and went into her room without knocking. She wasn't in bed. I panicked, thinking, *Oh God, not Mom, too.*

"Ebon?" Mom's voice came from behind me somewhere.

I turned around. From the hall I called out, "Mom?"

"In here, Ebon."

She sat in Dad's study curled up on the window seat, wrapped in Dad's nap blanket. He slept bunched up on the window seat sometimes. He covered up with the blanket his grandma had made him when he was my age. It smelled like him—all dried grass and mustardy.

Mom opened the blanket and I crawled into her lap. Kissing the top of my head, she whispered, "Missing him too?"

I hummed a response. I didn't want to talk. Warmed by her body heat, I could feel Mom and hear her heart beat. Dad was there too. I could smell him.

I dreamed we had all piled into the hammock like Mom, Dad, and I used to do on summer Wednesdays, when Samuel was away at swimming lessons and Joliet was doing her art class at the library. I fell asleep dreaming of the hot sun on my face and the creaking sway of the hammock in my ears.

Nothing Normal
About It

Mom gave us kids the order to go on with our lives as if nothing had gone wrong. Mom even made us breakfast and set out our school lunches like she did on every other Friday. I wanted to smash the paper bags she lined up on the counter until they turned into a gooey mush.

Joliet had the right attitude. She wore all black and refused to eat breakfast. I followed her lead and didn't eat anything. Samuel dived into a bowl of applesauce with pancake bits, but I couldn't watch. I went to find B. J.

Most mornings B. J. hung out in her tree house. After Dad built us a castle, her dad, who I had to call Mr. Taggert, insisted on making something for B. J. He tried to top Dad. B. J. had a real house in a tree. The place had everything—two rooms plus a porch, multipaned windows with shutters, a glass handle on the front door, and siding. Her mom (who let me call her Rita) even made a flower box and planted ivy in it, then hung it off the little porch. The place didn't even have a ladder. A staircase led up to the porch.

B. J. saw me coming across her yard and shouted from the porch, "You okay?"

What a dumb question. I didn't bother to answer her. I

just walked up the steps, sat down on the bench, and stared at her for being stupid.

"I'm sorry, Ebon." She held her arms out. "Need a hug?"

Her grandma Helen had to be the huggiest person in the world. Thanks to her, hugs became B. J.'s solution to everything. I didn't move, so I guess she figured I didn't like the idea. She sat next to me.

"What happened?"

"He fell asleep," I whispered.

"Did he hurt his head?"

"I don't want to talk about it."

"Okay." B. J. sat up in her I'll-take-charge way, then said, "Let's change the subject. Will they open Hamilton Hall tonight?"

I'd forgotten about Hamilton Hall. Only Dad could run the special effects. And that place meant more to Dad than Christmas presents did to Samuel. He lived all year for it. I couldn't let all Dad's hard work go to waste. I knew he kept a guidebook of all his haunting plans inside the house. He scribbled in it at night when he thought we were asleep. Okay, I'll admit it, I was almost as good a spy as Dad was. I'd seen the book sitting on a shelf or a ladder behind him when I made deliveries to Hamilton Hall. I enjoyed the surprises in Hamilton Hall too much to sneak a real peek at the plans. But now I had to.

"We've got to find Dad's book."

"We? Do what?" B. J. stammered. Ever since kindergarten she'd refused to go into Hamilton Hall. Back then she'd gotten lost in the dark and went into a fake dining room where a family of headless people ate a dinner of mushy brains (Dad called it the Food for Thought Room). That girl flew out of the house screaming like the devil was chasing her. We had to set an age limit after that.

"Come on"—I leaned into her—"the place won't be scary if we know all of Dad's tricks."

"But we have to find the book first."

"It's daylight. Besides, the place is only scary when Dad turns on all the special effects. The hidden doors and secret passages just make the place into a maze. Treat it like a life-size puzzle."

"Ebon, I still have nightmares about that place."

"Please." I squeezed her arm. "I have to do *something*."

B. J. stared at me. I could feel her arm shake in my hands. "Okay."

"Do we have a deal?" I held out my hand.

Mom called from below, "Ebon, Belinda Jane, we have to leave."

I got up to go, but B. J. grabbed me, asking, "What do we tell our parents?"

I thought on it a bit, then said, "We'll go to school, then cut out before the first bell and meet back at Hamilton Hall."

"That's a plan." B. J. and I shook hands, then headed for my driveway.

As soon as we got to school, B. J. and I ran down to the basement. I ducked into the boys' bathroom by the art room. She ducked into the girls'. I stood on the tank of the last toilet, then wiggled my way out the window. We came out onto the teachers' parking lot and cut through the trees in the park behind the school. From there, we caught a bus home. I grabbed Dad's keys from the hook by the phone in the kitchen and hightailed it to Hamilton Hall.

B. J. paced in the backyard. I stood by the door, hunting for the right key, saying, "Come on, B. J., it won't be scary in the daytime."

"Have you been in there?"

I hadn't. Dad never let us in. I felt like lying to her, but when I wandered around like an idiot after I opened the door, she'd know the truth. "No."

"I can't go."

B. J. looked like she would run home at the first creaking floorboard, so I said, "Just let me go in and have a look around. I'll come back and get you."

"Okay."

The back door sounded like the hull hatch of a sunken ship, it creaked so much, but Dad rusted the hinges on purpose. B. J. backed away. I peered inside. The first room looked like a dark closet—all the walls close in and painted black. I hated dark closets.

We had bats in our house, and I once pulled a pair of

shoes off the shelf in our hall closet only to find that a bat had nested in my left shoe! The thing flew right up in my face, and I flew right out of the house. I'm no screaming scaredy, but a bat in the face would make a soldier run.

Holding my breath, I stepped inside Hamilton Hall. The floorboard under my right foot sank, and *slam!* the door closed. I should have known better.

In a flash B. J. started pounding on the door. "Are you okay?"

All that pounding only freaked me out more. Here I stood in a pitch-black room with no windows, and B. J. drummed on the door like a Frankenstein monster locked in a dungeon.

"Cut it out!" I shouted. "Dad just rigged the door."

"You're okay?"

"Fine."

Actually, it felt like someone stood behind me, leaning over my shoulder. I got that feeling a lot when I went to the bathroom at night—like someone followed me there.

Dad said some folks feel the walls when they walk. I don't mean they touch them. He claims the heat off their body floats out, touches the wall, then comes back and taps them. I guess it's a trick some blind people use to help them navigate. Dad picked all of this up when he did research for a novel about a woman who goes blind in a car accident. I just wished I had a blind person there to help me get out of that room.

B. J. wasn't able to budge the door from her side, and I couldn't even find a handle.

"Should I go get help?" she asked.

"No, I'll figure it out." I put my hands out flat on the wall to feel for a secret panel or lever and tapped around with my feet to look for the same thing in the floor.

"Okay, Dad, where'd you hide the exit?" I asked the air. For a second I thought I heard static. Did Dad leave a walkie-talkie behind?

Groping around, I found one of Mom's gargoyles. The long tongue told me it had to be the one she made in two pieces so the tongue could grow longer (she called him Pinocchio Jr.). I gave the tongue a yank, and a door opened to my left. I couldn't see a thing.

"Did something move?" B. J. asked. She must've had her ear to the door.

"Yep. A door opened."

"What can you see?"

"Nothing."

"Why didn't we bring a flashlight?"

"Now you think of it." I stepped toward the door, tapping in front of me to test the floor for triggers (I could've used that blind lady's cane).

The hallway walls felt rough under my fingertips, like the paint had begun to peel. "Come on, Dad. There has to be a light switch here somewhere."

Down the hall on the right-hand side, behind the painting.

The words drifted into my head. I could've thought them, but they felt stiff and kind of weird—like a mental pair of new shoes.

Rushing forward, my hand on the wall, I bumped into the painting. Sure enough, right in the center, I found a light switch. Flicking it, I half expected to see Dad standing there smiling, but I only saw peeling paint, cobwebs (Dad imported spiders), and a dusty floor.

With the light on, I went back to the closet room and hunted for the door spring. Dad'd hidden it behind a baseboard. I found the panel with my fingers.

B. J. stood in the open doorway peeking in, but she did it while leaning back instead of forward. "Is it safe?"

"I told you, none of the equipment is turned on. There are only little surprises like closing doors and hidden light switches. It'll be okay."

I took B. J.'s hand. She felt safe enough to step inside. We headed down the hallway. "Where are we going to find this book of your dad's?"

"The control room."

"Where was that last year?"

"I have no idea." Dad never gave away his secrets. The hallway didn't have any other visible exits, so I had to hunt for a door one-handed. B. J. didn't want to let go of the other one.

"We won't find anything dead will we?"

"No." Dad went for realism but not homicide, not even

of bugs. Cripes, we couldn't kill spiders, because he wanted to relocate them to Hamilton Hall.

I wondered if I should ask out loud where to find the doors, but I still wasn't sure if I'd really heard anything the last time. It could've been a good guess. And how could Dad have told me where he'd hidden that switch anyway?

Besides, if I asked him out loud, B. J. would think I'd gone nuts. Or maybe just that I'd started to think out loud. "Where could that door be?" I said.

"Who knows with your dad. He probably put it in the ceiling."

Now there's an idea. Loud and clear.

"But it's not there, is it, Dad?"

"What?" B. J. turned to me.

I felt embarrassed. "It's not there, is it, bud?"

"Oh."

Nope.

My mind had taken a turn toward the funny farm. Worrying about Dad made me wish he could be there so hard that I thought I could hear him in my own head. Maybe if I talked about it, the thoughts would go away. Then again, did I want them to?

"What drained you?" B. J. asked. "You look all tired out."

"Just worried about Dad."

"Maybe we should go visit him."

"When we find the book."

I went faster, rubbing the wall for another secret latch, feeling like I had ice cubes in my chest. I'd never felt so scared. I wanted Dad there to tell me it'd be okay—or Mom walking with her arms around me like she did when she took me through the haunted house. She went through first and scouted everything out, then came back and took us kids through one at a time. She acted as our spirit guide, shielding us when things got too scary, hugging us when we panicked, but always letting us lead the way.

"Found it!" B. J. stuck her fingers into a crack in the wall, and a door sprang open to reveal a spiral staircase winding down into darkness. "I'm not going down there."

"Let's go get a flashlight, then go down."

"Right." B. J. ran to her tree house to get one. We never knew when we'd have to make a bathroom run back to the house at night. The place had electricity, but no john.

I stood there alone, feeling that shadow of a person behind me. "Are you here, Dad?"

Silence.

I spun in a circle. "Dad?"

"No, just me." B. J. held up a flashlight.

"Right." I took it, turned it on, then headed down the stairs.

The stairs stopped at a wall, but I found the switch really quickly, and we came out in the library. "Don't touch any books." I'd fallen into that trap enough times and been spun around into another room.

We hunted in one room, then another, sprung traps, fell into hidden holes, landed on piles of mattresses, and searched and groped for hours. I got so hungry even my spit tasted good. B. J. kept asking if we could give up, but I had to find the book.

After the thirteenth door leading into a brick wall, I'd had enough. Backing into the center of the room, I shouted, "Where is the darn book?"

B. J. stared at me like I'd gone nuts, but clear as if I'd thought it up myself, I heard, *All you had to do was ask.*

"So tell me!" I shouted.

Go in the kitchen, open the fridge, and take out the milk.

Laughing, I realized just how silly I was being for thinking Dad could really talk to me through my thoughts. Who did I think he was, Harry Houdini's mother? Dad said she'd promised to talk to Houdini from the grave.

"Who are you yelling at?" B. J. asked.

"Nobody. I'm just going goofy with hunger. Let's find a door leading out."

I tried to retrace our steps and that brought us back through the kitchen. Passing the fridge, I had the urge to open it, but what would that mean? Dad could talk to me? From where? Was he dead?

"Ebon, you're shaking."

"I'm just hungry," I told B. J. as I grabbed the fridge handle.

"Is that fridge hooked up?"

"Let's see."

Only a pitcher of milk sat inside.

"Milk." B. J. leaned in to grab it. "I'm so thirsty." When she tried to take the milk out of the fridge, the whole shelf came forward. As the shelf moved, a tray lowered from the top of the fridge. A key slid to the bottom of the tray. "Leave it to your dad." She shook her head.

Grabbing the key, I knew Dad had spoken to me. But how? I had to see him.

Making
Sure

All through the bus ride to the hospital B. J. tried to talk to me, get me to tell her what had happened, but I couldn't say anything. My thoughts spun around so fast that everything in the bus seemed to be spinning.

"Ebon, shouldn't we call your mom?"

I think I shook my head. I heard the driver say, "Fairfield Hospital."

Jumping up, I ran for the door. I had to sneak into Dad's room. All the slinking through Hamilton Hall had made me into an old pro at getting into secret places.

Alive and still asleep, Dad lay there in bed like he'd just checked in to a hotel for the night. Except for the bouquets of flowers surrounding his bed, his room could've been inside any Holiday Inn. I stood back and stared, afraid to approach him. A huge pot of planted flowers sat on his bed stand. *From Mom,* I thought. She knew how cut flowers made Dad sad.

He started snoring and I had to laugh.

I ran up and took his hand. Warm and soft, it felt like it did when he held mine. "You're okay."

Why wouldn't I be?

This time Dad spoke. He really spoke. I could hear him

as clearly as if he stood next to me. But his lips didn't move.

"What happened?" B. J. came closer.

"Didn't you hear that?"

"What?"

"Dad. He spoke to me."

"I'm calling your mom." B. J. rushed out of the room.

"I can hear you, Dad. Come on, wake up."

Wake up? When did I fall asleep?

Before I could answer Dad, the room got all wobbly. A nurse rushed in to get me out of there. I begged her to let me stay as I gripped the bar on Dad's bed to keep me steady. I'd heard Dad. I really had, but everything shrank into this little black dot before I had time to prove it.

Believing

I woke up in Mom's arms. She had me all tucked into a blanket in the hospital bed we shared. Seeing her rings, hearing her hum, smelling that dusty talcum powder scent that could only be hers, made me warm right up to the roots of my hair. I hugged her closer.

"Ebon." She kissed my ear.

"I heard Dad, Mom."

"That's what B. J. told me." The distant "oh, really" sound in her voice said she didn't believe me.

"He told me where to find all of the hidden tricks in Hamilton Hall."

"Look at me, sweetie." Mom nudged me to roll over. I did. "Dr. Parker says you haven't eaten all day. Now, running around on an empty stomach and the stress of all this with Dad made you think you heard him."

"I did!"

"Shhh." Mom rubbed my forehead, her face wet with tears.

"Is Dad . . ." Still asleep? Okay? Awake? I had no idea what to ask.

"He's still the same, Ebon." Mom wiped away her tears. Her hand shook as she rested it on the bed. I put my hand over hers to steady it.

Smiling, she said, "I can't stop shaking."

"Me either, on the inside." I patted my chest. Taking a breath, I asked, "Mom?"

She hummed to let me know she was listening. I didn't know what to say. I just wanted her to keep talking. I needed her to tell me everything would be okay. "What is it, Ebon?"

"Nothing." I really didn't know what to say.

Mom rubbed my shoulder. "It's okay, kiddo. We'll be okay."

"Are you sure?"

She looked at me, her eyes so dark they looked black—deep and safe like a familiar room. She didn't even blink as she said, "Yes, we will."

I believed her.

Dad had to be all right. If life were a picture, it'd be like cutting Dad out and leaving an empty hole. Seeing pictures with holes always made me lonely.

That evening Dr. Parker let us all see Dad. We stood beside him, holding his hands, rubbing his forehead, telling him how much we loved him (or tickling his feet—Joliet did that).

In my mind I saw Dad coming out of Hamilton Hall, the purplish horizon of dawn behind him, the die-hard fans of the place sleeping on the lawn to be there when he came out. They all clapped. He bowed, smiling, looking like he'd melt into the house if he got any happier.

Dad never really got credit for all the work he did. Every day he researched for another author who would stick only one name on the book that got published. And when the reviews came in and the critics praised the historical accuracy of the piece, they never mentioned Dad. The author got all the fame. Hamilton Hall was the one time Dad got to take all of the credit.

People had to see all of Dad's hard work. Hamilton Hall had to open, even if Dad couldn't be there. Mom, Joliet, and Samuel agreed. Giving Dad one more kiss, we all headed out for Hamilton Hall.

Daffodils
and Glimpses

The way Mom walked into Hamilton Hall and looked around like she had embarked on a hunt for a new home, I figured she knew something I didn't. "Do you know where the control room is?"

"Look for a daffodil."

"Why?" Joliet asked.

"It's corny," Mom warned as she turned a corner.

"Corn me!" we three shouted together.

"When your dad gave me our engagement ring, it hung in a bouquet of daffodils, and the card said, 'Here's the key to my heart.'" She used her isn't-this-doofy voice when she described the message on the card, then continued in her regular voice, "He always refers to the control room as the heart of his operation, so I'm guessing the lock will be behind a daffodil."

"That's ridiculous," Joliet said.

Which part, Jolie?

I wasn't going to give in this time. I figured Mom and Dr. Parker had it right. I had let my mind carry me away.

It's all true, you know. The daffodils and the ring and the lock. There were daffodils in a vase on the counter when your mom was on duty at the front desk of our dorm the night we met.

I'd heard that story before. I wasn't about to fool myself

this time. Dad couldn't put his thoughts into my head.

Mom found a painting of some crabby-looking lady holding a daffodil. As she moved the painting to get to the locked door I could see the lady better, and it was Mom in an old-fashioned dress.

Pretty good, huh? I used a projector to trace Mom's face onto an old painting.

I'm not giving in, I told myself as I gave Mom the key I'd found so she could unlock the door. Dad had made an old pantry into the control room. He had labeled all the drawers to keep track of the spare parts he stored inside. We searched inside them for Dad's code book. I wanted to ask Dad to tell me where he'd hidden the darn thing, but I was afraid that I'd hear his answer. I actually felt relieved when I heard Joliet shout, "Here it is!"

Joliet had found the book under a stack of floor plans in one of the cupboards. The book told us how to set up each trick Dad had created inside the house. We learned how to make a ghost float from a parlor to a dining room with film projectors rigged up on either side of the wall. B. J. and I ran trigger wires across hallways and between furniture so unsuspecting visitors would set creaking chairs, moaning doors, and an empty dress into motion.

Going from room to room, we set up everything Dad had created. We got so busy reading, rigging, and preparing that I forgot all about the extra voice in my head.

By nightfall we felt almost ready. Joliet and Samuel kept

their old roles. B. J. collected tickets, I ran the sound board at the back of the stage, and Mom played special effects wizard in the control room. No one seemed to notice the difference. Everyone came out as dazed, shaky, and psyched as they always did. The diehards camped out in front to listen to Samuel, roast marshmallows, and wait for dawn.

Seeing them there only reminded me that Dad wouldn't come out to take his bow, so I felt relieved when B. J.'s Mom came over.

"Hey, Ebon, I can run the board if you want to go through."

"Thanks," I said, standing up to go in.

Rita asked, "Want anyone to go through with you?"

I just wanted to get away from the growing crowd on the lawn, so I shook my head, then went inside by myself. Dad had outdone himself. Spirits slipped through walls, faint whisperings led you through secret passages to a ghostly meeting about a pirate raid, and a distressed mother of generations past roamed the halls for a missing child. I had my worries scared right out of me.

Stepping into a hallway, I caught a glimpse of a beat-up old conductor's hat. The man who wore it stood a head above the five people behind him. Dad?

I ran after him, but he was gone when I got around the corner. Did I just imagine him there? The rest of the way through Hamilton Hall I didn't even pay attention to the tricks, I just looked for Dad. I never so much as thought I caught a glimpse of him.

Castle
Rook

When I walked out the back door, I kept right on going. I needed to be closer to Dad but knew the nurses wouldn't let me see him so late at night. Everyone has a place that makes you think of all the time you've spent together. B. J. and I had her tree house. Dad and I had Castle Rook.

I got close enough to rub the walls of Castle Rook, but I couldn't go inside. I just sat down in front of the drawbridge, remembering our after-school ritual.

When I didn't have piano practice, I'd come home from school and run upstairs to feed Fred, my iguana. Dad would show up and sit on the banister. When he leaned back, he could rest his head on the slanted part of the ceiling, so it looked like he was just floating there above the open stairs.

I'd tell him about school. He'd tell me about all the weird little facts he'd found—like Thomas Jefferson didn't give public speeches after he became president, because he had a speech impediment, or Andrew Jackson drooled all the time, and they tried to get him kicked out of the Senate for it. I'd feed Fred, then we'd collect everybody for a little time in Castle Rook.

It was my favorite place in the world. I even kept a map
of it to show my friends.

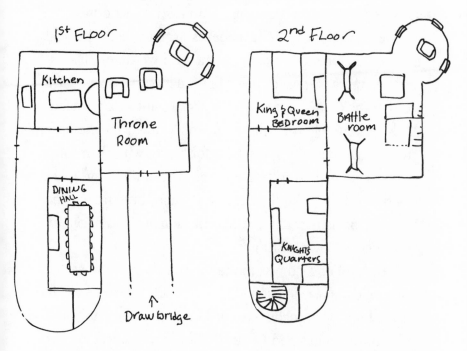

The castle was built out of those cement blocks you see in
cellars (ours was more like a cave with these drippy rock
walls—spooky). Two stories tall, Castle Rook—or Raven
Castle, as Samuel sometimes called it—had six rooms and
everything a good castle should: a throne room, a battle
room where we kept wooden horses and Styrofoam lances,
and two secret hiding places that weren't so secret anymore. We even had a kitchen, two bedrooms, and a dining
room. Dad built a well outside. The fireplaces worked, too,
but Mom or Dad had to be there for us to use them. Dad

built a watchtower inside. That was the only place with windows, because it was tough to keep a castle cool in the summer or warm in the winter with a lot of windows.

A few years back Mom made us armor out of the pull tabs of pop cans (even with all the pop we drank, it took her two years to collect the tabs). Each summer we gave tours of the castle, and it was just like a saint's day in a feudal kingdom, when all the serfs who worked for the king came to celebrate the special day for a saint with their ruler.

Dad said we had to trade off the part of the king. Joliet was the best at it. Well, she was a queen, but she did the grooviest British accent and had those *thous* and *oughts* of regal speech down just right.

Even funnier, Dad was too tall to stand up in the castle. Since he'd built it for us kids, he'd made the rooms only six feet high. That made him the kingdom giant who could sit on our enemies and fart until they surrendered.

We didn't always playact when we went to Castle Rook. We went there most every afternoon when school got out. We goofed off on the mats in the battle room, wrestling or whatever. Sometimes we played board games in the dining room or hide-and-seek. Every once in a while we'd just work on making things for the castle. Mom built a loom, and we all pitched in to make rugs and tapestries.

Castle Rook was the place. Joliet became Lady Divia. She took archery lessons at the U of M, so she could shoot an arrow through the rings Dad had hung from the trees.

Samuel became Sir Obb, and he loved making goofy weapons out of anything he found lying around. He had a slingshot carved out of an old flour scoop he'd found in an antique store for a quarter because it had a crack in it. I became Sir Harout (said without the *T*) and I helped out. I helped Sir Obb test his weapons and Lady Divia make her arrows.

I guess we were all still these things, but with Dad in a coma, it didn't feel right to go into Castle Rook. I couldn't throw rocks out the turret window (pebbles, really) and hit the hall window so Dad could open it to shout, "Five o'clock and all is well!" or "It's six o'clock and the banquet will be served in the hunting lodge"—that's our real house—"in one half hour!" I couldn't scream, "Lord Lucas! We're being invaded!" and know Dad would come running, Styrofoam sword swinging.

I couldn't imagine going to Castle Rook knowing Dad wasn't along, or inside the house hunting down the reasons why the U.S. has one of the only cultures in the world where women shave their legs. Don't get me wrong. Nobody could call me a daddy's boy. I knew there were lots of kids who didn't have a dad around, but mine had always been there. Sure, he was distracted a lot, but my dad was still a cool guy. I would've thought so even if he weren't my dad, and I wanted him back. But imagining him in places he didn't exist and hearing him when he couldn't even speak wouldn't do the trick. I had to pray and wait for him to heal, just like everyone else.

Rip van Winkle Disease

That weekend we cuddled a lot and looked at family pictures, cried, played Monopoly, visited Dad, and ate enough junk food to give a horse a heart attack. Waiting with my family almost seemed bearable, but going to school felt like being turned inside out.

Teachers told me how sorry they were to hear that my dad had fallen ill, then piled on the homework until my book bag felt heavy enough to be filled with rocks. My mind crowded up with instructions and due dates.

The other kids kept asking me stupid questions—Is your dad okay? What happened? The dumbest stories started. One said Dad had gone hunting for distant relatives in a graveyard and got struck by lightning. Gilbert Redding wanted to know if my dad had really been abducted by aliens then deposited next to the cherry in the big spoon sculpture outside the Walker Art Center. I hated all the questions and the stupid looks.

I wanted to go back to being plain old Ebon Jones. Not the mysterious Samuel Jones, who could recite the J and K sections of the Minneapolis white pages. Not the artistic Joliet, who could make a human being look like a tree with only felt, thread, and a sewing machine. Not Mom, who could make a rock into a fire-spitting, pointy dude who looked as though he'd pop up at any moment and use the crooked little wings she gave him to fly.

And certainly not Dad. I'd never built a castle or designed an entire Western-town play set. I could barely remember all twenty-five of my spelling words, let alone try to think up the names, dates of birth, terms of office, and little-known facts about each president of the United States and France. I wouldn't know the first place to look if some author asked me to find out when jelly beans were invented. No, I was plain old Ebon, and it used to bother me a lot that I was the normal kid in a really odd family, but when Dad feel asleep, I became desperate for the old days when everybody ignored me.

Not everybody. B. J. never ignored me. No, B. J. was space shuttle material. Next to Dad, she was the best friend I had in the world. After school sometimes, we'd run through our skateboard tricks on the playground. We were working on our 360-degree kick flips that Monday. If I didn't concentrate on my moves, I'd end up with broken bones, so I kept my mind on getting them down. The mind bending kept me from dwelling on Dad and those stupid thoughts. I took a mean turn and landed square.

Waiting for my next spin, I noticed Samuel hanging out at the other end of the steps playing Hacky Sack with his buddies. They smiled and laughed. What did Samuel have to laugh about, I wondered. I stepped closer to listen.

I heard one kid ask, "What's wrong with your dad, anyway?"

Samuel said, "He's got Rip van Winkle disease." The others laughed, but that crack put my rage into overdrive. I ran at him—full tilt.

I knocked Samuel to the ground. Shaking him by the shoulders, I shouted, "How could you say that?"

Mr. Haffner, a crossing guard from down the block, pulled me off and dragged me into the office. Mr. Haffner went on and on about appropriate school yard behavior. Samuel just sat there with his hands in his lap like he'd never done anything wrong in his life. Mrs. Gilford came in and said she'd called Mom, and asked Mr. Haffner to join her in the hall. They stood under the clock whispering and sputtering about Dad. I wished for a volume control on life so I could just turn it up whenever someone tried to hide something from me by whispering.

Next thing I knew, Mom arrived and dragged us off to a psychologist. She said we needed to work through our emotions. She accepted no excuses for being cruel to each other. How about cruelty to Dad? Samuel was being totally mean to Dad. That little twerp needed a psychologist, not me.

Mom picked a total drip to be our shrink. With a name like Dr. Ventro, he sounded as if he'd walked straight out of a comic book. Tall and thin, he reminded me of Auntie Em's hired hand before he turned into the Tin

Woodsman in the *Wizard of Oz* movie. He had breath that smelled like he'd been sucking on an air freshener, and he always had little globs of spit in the corners of his mouth. They never fell out, so he wasn't literally a drip, but he bugged me.

His office looked like the playground at McDonald's, with a miniature jungle gym and piles of toys all over the place. We sat in a ring of chairs on a stupid rug with the alphabet on it. The shrink sat in a little kid's chair, so his bony knees came so high up he could've had a kneecap sandwich.

Samuel still hadn't stopped whining about the fact that I'd knocked him down. The psychologist had Samuel tell his whole stupid story. Of course Samuel retold it word for word and included a description of body language just to show off. At the end he said, "All I did was say Dad had Rip van Winkle disease."

Seeing Samuel shake as he told the story made me realize how totally out of control I'd been. I could've really hurt the kid. What a creep. (Me, not Samuel.)

Dr. Ventro asked, "Why did that make you so angry, Ebon?"

Samuel interrupted, "Dad told me that's what's wrong with him."

"Dad didn't tell you anything," Joliet snapped.

"He did too."

Could Dad have spoken to him, too? All that time I'd

been trying to shut out that voice in my head, and I could've been talking with Dad?

Mom said, "Now, Samuel, you know your father can't talk."

"That's all right, Wynne," Dr. Ventro said as he got up and started walking around the tiny red chair he'd been sitting in. "Perhaps Samuel did hear his father speak to him. Children in this type of situation frequently invent things that help them cope."

"I didn't invent anything!" Samuel insisted. "Dad said it. He said, 'It's okay. I just have a slight case of Rip van Winkle disease.'"

It sounded like Dad. He would say that about himself. I could see him sitting at the table in Kingston's fluttering his eyes, saying, "It only hurts when I blink."

Joliet said, "That's so stupid."

"Now, Joliet, what's wrong with saying your father has Rip van Winkle disease?" the shrink asked, as if Samuel had said Dad had cancer.

Mom giggled. It was one of those I-tried-to-hold-it-back types of giggles that sputters out. "Come on, Jolie. You know Dad would think that was hilarious."

In that instant Dad's voice came back

I thought it was a gas.

I really could hear Dad speak. No shrink could convince me otherwise. I got up, saying, "I have to go to the bathroom."

"Right now?" Mom asked.

Remembering Dad's favorite line, I said, "Sorry, my bladder doesn't have a watch."

I heard Dad laugh. Samuel started to giggle.

"Did you hear that?" I mouthed to Samuel. He leaned forward, his eyes bulging. Was he confused or shocked?

"It's okay, Wynne," Dr. Ventro said. "Let him go."

Mom squeezed my hand as I went for the door. Dr. Ventro started talking about grief, and I motioned for Samuel to follow me. He popped up, shouting, "Gotta whiz!"

He ran for the door, and I hurried out with him. We rushed into the bathroom. Crowding Samuel into a stall, I asked, "Did you hear Dad laughing just a minute ago?"

He shrugged.

"You just said you heard Dad!"

"I did. He came into my dream last night." Samuel had started to whine as if I'd scared him.

"But not out loud?"

"What, do you think I'm nuts?" He laughed.

No, I was apparently. I'd done it again. Made myself believe in magic tricks. I sent Samuel back into Dr. Ventro's office to tell Mom I'd gone home.

A
Ghost?

Yeah, let me go crazy. What a great idea. The shrink's big solution to all our problems was to have a Dad ban. We wouldn't go see him for the time being. We were all supposed to pick up our daily routine—Joliet would go back to her archery class, Samuel would start up with the chess club again, and I had to go back to piano lessons. Time away from Dad would help us all calm down, or so Dr. Ventro thought. Mom said the hospital would call if anything changed, and we'd be at Dad's side faster than Superman in rush hour.

I pegged it all for a hoax. Mom and the shrink thought Dad would die. They'd given up and wanted us to be without Dad for a while so we could get used to the idea of Dad being gone for good. I knew their tricks and I wasn't going to fall for them.

By the next day I had a plan for sneaking into Dad's room through the window, but Mom didn't let me go to school. The stupid shrink said I needed to sort through my feelings so I could talk about them without getting so mad I wanted to hurt people. He even planned on coming to our house the next day because he thought talking in a home environment would be more comfortable for me.

Yeah, right. What I really needed was to be with Dad. Mom didn't agree. She said I needed some cooling-off time.

Cooling off? Who needed to cool off? I wasn't a jet engine about to overheat. I was a guy who needed to see his Dad. But I guess they had it partly right. I mean, I did hear voices. Relaxing might help get rid of them.

I stared at the cracks in the ceiling until I dozed off. When I woke up, I thought I saw Dad standing at the top of my stairs in his flying-toaster housecoat. It hung open; I could see his T-shirt and boxers. He wore only one sock.

I sat up and he vanished. I screamed. Mom came running.

"I'm going crazy!"

She came to my bed and cuddled me close to her, whispering, "No, you're not."

"I saw Dad. I really saw him. I heard him again yesterday, too. In the doctor's office. He said . . . he said . . . he spoke to me."

"Ebon, Dr. Ventro says it's normal to see loved ones we miss and hear them too. It's normal."

"But he was here."

"I'm sure you saw him, Ebon, but he wasn't here."

I believed her for a while. Exactly fourteen hours. Something woke me up at around one o'clock in the morning. Listening, I heard the door to the stairwell leading up to my attic close. To be sure I wasn't going crazy, I went downstairs.

Everything on the third floor was still except the water running in the toilet. I walked through the Shroom Forest—a reading area closed in by bookshelves with a ton of brown beanbag chairs (shrooms). I wanted to snuggle down with Dad and a good book, something from England so he could do a British accent.

I peeked into Samuel's room. He slept at the wrong end of the bed, his covers strewn all over like a pile of dirty laundry. Coated in mess, his room would be a challenge to Mary Poppins. The least he could do was clean his room, the little creep. How could he just sleep like that?

I went down to the second floor, stood in the hallway, and listened. The toilet was running down there, too. Mom had her windows open. I could hear the curtains blowing in the wind and a bunch of noisy birds chirping away. But there was also a humming sound. A low hum from a machine. I would've thought it was a fish tank if we still had one, but Fred ate Samuel's fish.

I walked toward the sound. Dad's office door hung open, and I could see the blue green glow of Dad's computer screen through the crack. I gave the door a little push, expecting to see Mom working on something, but no one was there.

I sat down in Dad's chair wishing it were still warm the way it felt after he'd just gotten up. I had to give the pedal underneath the seat a few kicks so I could reach the computer. I thought I'd give Dad a little help by doing some research. He was probably really hungry for some juicy facts. I could take them to the hospital and tell him everything I'd learned. He might even wake up to ask a question or two.

I tried to think of something groovy to hunt for, but nothing came to mind; then I saw the tower of pop cans Dad had built up, and decided to find out when pop was invented. Hooking into Dad's encyclopedia database, I put "pop" in as a search word, and a bunch of links for pop music came up.

I heard Dad's voice, as smooth and calm as if he'd told me the answer to a math question. He said, *Try soda.*

I didn't hear that, or so I told myself. Like Mom had said, I only wanted to hear Dad. He didn't actually say anything. How could he?

But I put in *soda,* anyway. I remembered that my cousins from Oregon made fun of me when I said "pop," so I figured most people used the word *soda.* I also put in *history* to refine the search. A bunch of cough syrups sites came up.

"Cough syrup?" I asked myself out loud.

"That's right. Pop flavoring was sweetened cough syrup, then they mixed it with soda water."

I didn't know enough about the history of pop even to imagine that connection. Dad had to be speaking to me. The sound of his voice came from behind me, so I turned around.

Dad sat in the window seat. The glow from the screen went right through him and shone on the window, but it also lit him up like Bob Cratchit in a Scrooge movie.

I stumbled out of the chair. Dad stood up; his face looked so still and scary. I started to run. He ran so fast I felt sure he'd catch me. I told myself not to look as I sped down the front steps, then out the door, but I had to look—to see if he had really been there. Looking over my shoulder, I caught a glimpse of Dad standing in the study window, still glowing, his eyes all black, his fingers long and white as they touched the glass.

On the
Run

There was nothing I could do but run and hope Dad couldn't follow me. As I ran down the middle of the street I thought it must've all been a dream, but I could feel tiny rocks jabbing the bottoms of my feet, and it sounded like those chirpy birds laughed at me.

Cutting across B. J.'s lawn, I tapped at her window. She yanked it open, saying, "Jeez, you almost made me peel out of my skin."

"I saw him."

"Who?"

Seeing her blink at me, half asleep, I figured she'd never believe me. Why should she? I crawled past her to go for the phone by her bed to tell Mom I'd gone totally nuts. Then I thought, *What if I did see Dad? What if he was a ghost?*

I said to B. J., "He could've died and that was his ghost. Oh, man, I can't call. You call!" I threw the phone at her. It landed on the bed.

"What are you talking about?" B. J. asked, rubbing her face to wake up.

"Dad, I saw Dad. He was all blue and glowing, just like one of his ghoulies from Hamilton Hall."

"You're making this up!"

"Would I be here if I made it up?"

B. J. dropped down onto her bed and covered her face with her pillow. I thought I'd scared her too, then she said, "This is not funny, Ebon Jones!"

"Funny?" I sat next to her. "You think I'm kidding?"

B. J. sat up. "This is the worst practical joke ever. How can you be mad at your brother for the Rip van Winkle crack if you'd do something like this?"

"No way!" I stood up. "This is no joke! I saw him. Twice!"

B. J. leaned forward, looking at me like she was scoping for wood ticks. "You aren't lying." I shook my head, and she sat back, her face a little paler. "Wow, I hope you're just going crazy."

"Me, too." Sad, I felt ready to cry.

The phone rang. We both dived for the floor. We lay there, our chins buried in the shag carpeting as the phone kept ringing.

"Belinda Jane?" her grandma Helen called down the stairs. "It's Wynne Jones. Is Ebon down there?"

"Oh, no. Oh, please God, no." I started pacing because I was sure Dad had died.

B. J. picked up the phone. "Wynne?" She listened to Mom, then said to me, "Ebon, she heard you go ballistic and tear out of the house and figured you'd come here."

"Dad's dead," I whispered to myself.

B. J. started shaking when she told my mom, "Ebon thinks . . . he's afraid Luke's dead." B. J. hung up the phone, then came to give me a hug. "Your mom's coming. She's coming, Ebon."

Grandma Helen came down to see what was up, and a few seconds later my mom arrived. She must have flown over. Sitting down on the bed, she drew me to her. "Ebon, if something happened to your father, the hospital would call us."

"What if they didn't have the time? What if they just didn't want to ruin our sleep and decided to wait until morning to tell us?"

"They wouldn't do that, Ebon. They know how much Dad means to us."

"But I saw him. I saw his ghost."

Mom tried to tell me it was all a dream, but I saw Grandma Helen hugging B. J. and I heard her say, "Knowing Luke Jones, he'd find a way to go home, dead or not."

He Said
"Cough Syrup"!

I couldn't go back to sleep. I sat in my bed glaring at the staircase. I jumped every time my curtains moved or the headlights of a passing car cast a shadow on my wall.

I tried the reciting-the-presidents trick. That made me more nervous. I felt like I'd been thrown inside the scariest movie ever, then the phone rang. I jumped out of bed knowing it had to be about Dad. I hated the way the waiting made my skin sting as if it'd just touched an exposed wire in an extension cord. I'd done that and hated even the thought of reliving it.

I heard someone charging up the stairs.

"Ebon!" Mom pounded on the door. "The hospital just called. We've got to go."

"What happened?" I yanked the door open. "Is Dad okay?"

Mom smiled, waving her hands in the air. "They think he said something."

"He talked? He talked!" We jumped around the room. Joliet and Samuel showed up. We spread the good news, then practically flew down to the car.

Dr. Parker met us at the nurses' station wearing a trench coat. I could see her sweatpants poking out from under the bottom hem. "False alarm," she said, her voice a low rumble.

"What do you mean?" Mom asked, almost growling.

"The nurse thought he said something about cough syrup, but I've checked in on him. His vital signs haven't changed. His pupils are nonreactive. He's still in a coma."

"Cough syrup?" I muttered.

"What, Ebon?" Mom asked.

"Did you say 'cough syrup'?" I asked.

"Yes, but she must have been mistaken." Dr. Parker led Mom toward the door, saying something about a special head doctor coming in from the Mayo Clinic. I slipped past them to go see Dad.

His skin looked pale like the lining of a clam. I took his hand, still warm to the touch. "Dad?" I whispered real close to his ear. "Tell me about pop, Dad. Please tell me."

He didn't so much as twitch. "I heard you, Dad." I squeezed his hand. "I heard you."

Mom came in. Putting her hands on my shoulders, she kissed me, then said, "We have to go, Ebon."

"I heard him, Mom. He did say 'cough syrup.'"

"Just now?" Mom practically shouted it as she pointed at Dad.

"No, at home. That's why I ran out. I saw him in the study. He told me pop started out as cough syrup."

"Oh, Ebon," She held her heart as if it beat too fast. "Honey, you just thought you saw your dad."

"What about the cough syrup? The nurse said she heard him say it, and so did I."

"It's just a coincidence, Ebon. Nothing more." She patted my back. "Give your dad a kiss."

I leaned forward. Kissing him on the ear, I whispered, "I know you were there, Dad. Please come back."

Mom gave Dad a kiss on the lips. Pushing his hair back behind his ear, she said, "Sleep well, my prince."

Dad, the Living Ghost

The ghost of a living person—what a cuckoo idea, but so was seeing and hearing someone who slept in a hospital bed miles away. Looney Tunes. Mom took us home and tucked us into bed, but I snuck right out and went straight to B. J.'s tree house. The sun hadn't come up yet, so I got the flashlight out of a kitchen drawer. When I shone it on her bedroom window, she poked her head out. I flashed the light on the grass in front of her. She crawled out of the window, then ran up to the tree house.

"What happened? I heard you guys leave," she said.

"Dad really did speak."

"What?"

"I heard him. When he was in the study. He told me pop started out as cough syrup, then the hospital called. A nurse heard him say 'cough syrup.'"

"Really?"

"It's like your grandmother said, no matter what, Dad'll find a way home."

"Utterly unbelievable." B. J. slid down the wall. "But it doesn't surprise me with your dad. What are you going to do?"

"He showed up when I needed some help. He told me

how to get through Hamilton Hall. And last night, when I was looking for answers on the Internet, I got stuck and he came to help me out."

"Wow."

"So I need to find something else he can help me out with."

"Like what?"

"I don't know."

"I know, I know!" B. J. waved her arms around as if they'd become dancing snakes. "What is the name of a male singer who sings higher than a tenor? I heard that one on the radio the other day."

We sat staring at the walls waiting for Dad to show up. "A male singer who sings higher than a tenor, Dad." I repeated her question in case Dad didn't hear her. Nothing.

"Maybe it's because he doesn't know?" B. J. suggested.

"Okay." I stood up, thinking Dad could hear me better. "Tell me, Dad, why did Attila the Hun die?"

"Why did he die?" B. J. asked.

"I can't tell you, then Dad will know I know."

"Now he does anyway." B. J. shrugged.

"Huh!" I slumped to the floor in exhaustion. B. J. and I kept it up until we fell asleep. Her mom found us there a few hours later. "Belinda Jane!"

B. J. and I both jumped. B. J.'s hair hung in her face. "Mom?"

Rita turned around to shout over the edge, "I found them!" Looking at us, she asked, "What are you two doing sleeping up here?"

"Um . . . um," B. J. fumbled.

"Never mind," Rita laughed. "Just tell somebody where you're going next time. We've been hunting all over for you. And you"—she pointed at me—"doesn't your mother have enough to worry about without you running off in the middle of the night?" B. J.'s mom sure could be mean when she got mad.

"Sorry, ma'am."

"Don't 'sorry' me. Apologize to your mother." She shooed me to the stairs. "Get on home." As I took the first step she kissed me on top of the head. "Love you, kiddo."

"See you soon, Ebon!" B. J. shouted over the edge.

I dragged myself down to the ground. My muscles tight and sore, it felt like I'd slept on a pile of my old toy trucks. As I came into the kitchen, Mom stood by the sink washing dishes. Samuel sat at the table digging through a new box of cereal for the prize inside. Dad always got out the big popcorn bowl and dumped the cereal into it to hunt for the prize, but Samuel preferred to half destroy the box by sticking his arm down inside to root around.

Mom bellowed like a drill sergeant, "Get over here, boy!"

"Yes, ma'am." I hurried to her side.

Hugging me and giving me a shake, Mom asked, "Where have you been?"

"I spent the night in B. J.'s tree house."

"You go AWOMK one more time and I'm putting a tracking device in your oatmeal. You'll swallow that sucker and I'll never lose track of you."

AWOMK—that's Momspeak for "absent without Mom's knowledge." "I'm sorry I didn't let you know where I was."

Mom deposited a blob of suds on my nose. "That's just it, Roving Boy. I know about your escape routes. I heard you leave last night." She pointed to the door. "That door makes a creak only a mother can hear."

I laughed.

"And Mrs. Gilford called to tell me you'd cut school."

"You knew about that?"

Mom raised her eyebrows. "I have my spies."

"I'm just trying to find a way to make Dad come back."

Mom pulled me close. "I know, Ebon. That's why I've given you a little room to roam, but don't abuse the privilege."

"I won't."

"Good. And do one more thing for me." Leaning over, Mom added in a whisper, "Don't tell anyone what you saw, Ebon."

"They'll think I'm nuts?" I mumbled, resting my head on Mom's arm.

I saw her close her eyes as she said, "No. I know that Samuel will believe you and Joliet will only get mad."

"And the kids at school will call the *National Sun Inquirer*."

Mom laughed, "Just like your father. Humor at all times."

I was being serious, but it didn't pay to tell Mom that. She was doing damage control. If I told Samuel, he'd be up every night waiting for Dad's ghost to show. She'd never get him to go to bed. Joliet would hate me for being so stupid.

Not B. J.'s grandma Helen—she believed in ghosts. She'd lived in a haunted house when she was eight. She had often played with a neat girl who wore ringlet curls, but it turned out she'd been dead for thirty years. The only trouble was the ghost would cry in the night, then one time the ghost walked into Helen's parents' bedroom to tell them someone had left the stove on. They moved out the next week.

Maybe that was it. Dad had to warn us about something. No, that didn't seem right. Ghosts often come back because they've left something unfinished. Maybe he felt like he had to stay around to help Mom raise us kids. Dad did schedule our lives around his research, but he always said being a father had to be the best part of his life. And he couldn't let go of it. That thought made me feel loved and guilty at the same time.

I'd gotten lost in my thoughts, so Mom had to call me back to our kitchen, "Ebon?"

"Yeah?"

"You ready to talk things out with Dr. Ventro?"

"Is he coming today?" If you'd asked me if I'd rather eat hot nails or see Ventro again, I'd have to think about it.

"Yep."

My moans told her how I really felt, so she said, "How about a picnic to warm you up to the idea. A good picnic can prepare you for any event."

Samuel sat up, asking, "Did I hear a rumor of a picnic?"

"Would you like to make it a fact, Samuel?" Mom turned around to face the table.

Samuel jumped up as he shouted, "Sure! I'll go get a blanket." He ran for the back stairs. "Make a hole, man on a mission." He pushed his way past Joliet as she came down.

"Can we go see Dad first?" Joliet asked.

Mom bowed her head. "No, honey, Dr. Ventro thinks it would be best—"

Joliet cut her off, "Who cares what Dr. Jerko thinks! He's my father. I want to see him."

"Jolie, please, I know you're upset."

"You don't seem to be. You just keep right on with your life like Dad's off to the dentist." Joliet moved in closer, the veins in her neck bulging out. If I hadn't felt her anger in my chest like a strange source of heat, I would've laughed at how much she looked like Fred casting his tongue out for a fly.

She almost growled when she asked, "Why, Mom? You know something you're not telling us?"

"What's that supposed to mean, Joliet?"

"I think you know. You know he isn't coming back. You're not tied in knots waiting for something good to happen. You're all calm and resolved. You think he's already dead!"

Joliet had it all wrong. I'd heard Mom crying as she talked with her sister, Aunt Rachel. Seen how she gripped the steering wheel for strength when the parents at school asked how Dad was. I knew how she jumped whenever the phone rang.

Mom stared at Joliet, her eyes looking as glossy as polished stones.

It felt like Dad stood there beside me, holding my hand. He wanted me to tell both of them he was there and everything would be all right.

Lacing her fingers together under her chin as if she wanted to pray, Mom said, "Promise me this—you won't guess how I'm feeling and I won't pretend to know what you're going through."

Joliet smiled, but it looked like a backward one to me. One of those lip curls that means hate, not happiness. She said to Mom, "So you do have feelings?"

Mom turned her head as if she was trying to hold herself back. "I'm going to walk outside now, Joliet. If you want to know how I really feel, you'll calm down, then come outside and talk with me—not at me."

Mom walked out. I saw Samuel peeking into the kitchen from the main stairs, but he went back up when the screen door flapped closed. Joliet just paced the room, muttering to herself. I wanted to say something, but my emotions had my brain all twisted and noodly. I felt like yelling at her for being so mean to Mom, but I saw the tears in Joliet's eyes. I knew how she hurt. There was no way out of the hole our family had fallen into unless Dad came back.

A Picnic
(Dad Style)

I wanted Dad to come and fix everything so bad I could see the outline of him bending over to look out the window as Joliet stepped outside. I could imagine the wavy lines of his housecoat draping over Samuel's science experiment, see the spikes of his light brown hair—a sandpaper haircut, as he called it.

If he had really been there, he would've asked me to open the window so we could hear what they were saying, so I did. I had to get all my weight behind a good shove to push that window open. A pesky fly buzzed around as I leaned toward the screen to hear what they said to each other, so their words sounded staticky.

Mom stood by Castle Rook playing with the frayed edges of our family flag, which hung down from the roof. Joliet must've been sitting down next to the house. I couldn't see her, and her voice sounded like she was speaking up from a tunnel in the ground. "I didn't mean to hurt you."

"Yes, you did." Mom kept facing the castle. "You wanted to see the pain, know I hurt as much as you do."

"You make me sound awful."

"I make you sound human, Jolie. It's no fun hurting

alone." Mom put her back to the castle wall, then slid to the ground. She looked like a kid, with her hands tucked between her legs, her shoulders below her kneecaps.

"So what's the deal, Mom? Why the stone-faced act?"

Mom closed her eyes, then lifted her brows—her I'm-an-idiot look. "I listened to Dr. Ventro. He said keeping up appearances would help you kids."

Laughing, Joliet said, "Dweeb."

Mom shouted, "Benzildug!"

That's our family word for a real jerk—it means the person's stupid, ugly, boring, cruel, and probably smells bad. I would've bet a year's supply of s'mores that declaring him a benzildug meant Mom would call off the meeting and we'd be rid of that guy.

"Pork-bellied fool!" Joliet yelled.

Mom laughed. Her whole body started to jiggle. Her laughter started out all crisp and bouncy like the sound fall leaves make when you run through a pile of them. It grew deeper, and her jiggle turned into a shake—she started crying. Joliet, too. She crawled over to Mom. They snuggled up together, bawling. All it took was seeing one tear and I began spouting water.

Mom halted all the waterworks when she stormed inside, shouting, "Knights and Ladies!" Opening the laundry chute door, she bellowed, "Knights, prepare for battle upon Picnic Glade!"

Samuel came thundering down the back stairs. Joliet went to the fridge to hunt down sandwich stock—twelve-grain bread, pickles, peanut butter, jelly, salami, tuna with mayo, lettuce, mustard, bananas, potato chips. I went for the small ladder to retrieve our new picnic basket (our kitchen cupboards go all the way up to the ten-foot ceiling on one wall, so it was a big climb). Mom got started on a pasta salad, and together we were well stocked and out the door in an hour.

Picnic Glade was a spot on a hill in the park behind our place. We went out the gate in our backyard, ran up a hill, and we were at the picnic glade, but Samuel had to go first, his sword blazing, to ward off any lurking thieves or sandwich-hungry dragons. I'd done that when I was his age too, but I thought it was silly, especially without Dad there to be the dragon (maybe it was wishful thinking).

Whenever we went on a picnic, Dad would always find a way to disappear before we got outside. He'd be waiting somewhere on the hill—ready to pounce. That was how our old picnic basket met its end. Dad jumped out of a juniper bush and tackled Mom. They went tumbling down into the valley with the picnic basket and rolled to a stop just feet from the creek. Dad had potato salad mashed into his hair and spotting his shirt. Mom looked like she'd tie-dyed her white shirt with grape juice. They laughed, but the old picnic basket had been reduced to tatters.

As I sat on Picnic Glade with everyone in our family but Dad, I remembered how we'd had to skip the picnic and take a trip through the drive-thru at Burger Chef. Dad refused to go get the car, so we walked through. I was so embarrassed. Joliet refused to join us and waited at the picnic table in the park.

The drive-thru dude put all our food into kid's-meal sand pails because he thought Dad was so goofy-cool. We ate in the sandbox and built a colony for the ants that came to eat the crumbs we dropped. The meal turned out to be pretty fun all around, but I got sand in my underwear (there's nothing worse than sand-butt).

Watching Samuel mush his ring-macaroni salad into the shape of a fish instead of eating it, I thought about how Dad did everything in a whirligig fashion. We'd start out in one place with a plan (a picnic), he'd do something goofy (go tumbling down the hill with Mom), we'd end up twisting and turning (walking through a drive-thru) to a whole new destination (dinner in a sandbox with a colony of ants). Dad was a classic.

I had the best rib muscles of any kid in kindergarten because I'd laughed so much at my Dad—no, *with* my Dad. He was totally serious when he was alone, so you'd have to be with him for him to do anything funny. The closer I got to being a teenager, the more I thought about how totally against the world my Dad was. He did everything his own way. After Dad put the Christmas ornaments up in June because he wanted the Christmas spirit to last all year, Mr. Taggert said Dad would paint his house pink just to be different from his neighbors. Mr. Taggert might have been on to something there, but a plain old picnic didn't seem right.

No
Denying It

We sat on the picnic glade and ate our sandwiches (mine was peanut butter and pickles—I decided to try something new) and ring-macaroni salad with peas and tiny shrimp.

We watched other people while we ate. I kept my eye on a group of Boy Scouts looking for their troop leader, stared at a man with plaid pants and a striped shirt, then watched a guy with purple hair put bubbles in the water fountain before I realized I was actually trying to find Dad in the park. I knew it was a hopeless, stupid thing to do, but I just kept right on looking.

"Ebon, Ebon!" Mom pulled me out of my search. "Go back to the house and get the Jell-O out of the fridge."

"I'll go!" Samuel got up to make a run for the fence.

"No, I'm going." I pushed past Samuel. It felt good to go home. Being in the park with all those people made me lonely.

I opened the back door to go in for the Jell-O and there, sitting on the floor, his bony knees sticking up in the air, his slippers scattered on the floor, was Dad. His hair all mussed up like he'd been hanging upside down again, he wore his smiley-face T-shirt and hip-pocket jean shorts. I'd seen them in pictures of his college days, but Mom said she'd burned them while Dad was skinny-dipping in the St. Croix River.

I froze. Dad scrambled to his feet, shouting, *"Don't run."*

I could hear him (he spoke loud enough to make me jump). I could see him (right down to the hair on his legs) as well as everything behind him—he was still a little see-through.

"Da—?" I couldn't even get the word out, he scared me so.

"It's me." He crouched down so we were looking eye to eye. I'd inherited Mom's short genes. Samuel was taller than me and I was two years older. *"It's just Dad, Ebon."*

I ran out of the house so fast I didn't even catch it from the screen door when I left it flapping in the wind. Out of breath and sweating like a glass filled with iced tea, I reached the top of the hill. "Mom, Mom, come here and look!" I pointed at the window.

Everyone scrambled to get up and have a look. They squinted. Mom asked, "What is it?"

Samuel leaned into me, then shouted, "It's Dad!" Bouncing on his tiptoes, he said, "I can see him looking out the window at us." Samuel waved.

Joliet and Mom came closer, almost squeezing me. By the amazed look on their faces I knew they could see him too.

"This isn't possible." Mom started to pace.

"Is that really Dad?" Joliet asked.

"One way to find out!" Samuel ran down the hill.

By the time we got to the kitchen, Dad had disappeared again. Samuel and Joliet went through the house calling for him. Mom did the shooting-gallery duck routine in the kitchen—walking from the dishwasher to the fridge, then back again. She mumbled to herself. I sort of looked around for Dad, but I was more worried about Mom; she had started to come a little unglued.

"This isn't possible, Ebon."

"I saw him, Mom."

Mom spoke more to herself than to me when she said, "He's in a coma."

"And he's here. I saw him before, too."

Mom shouted at the ceiling, "Luke! Can you hear me? What in the world are you doing?"

"He wore his smiley shirt and those goofy shorts you burned up."

"This is too strange."

The phone rang. Mom and I jumped like the floor had suddenly become electrified. If the caller had news about Dad, I wanted to hear it too, so I ran for the phone in the hall.

I missed the first part of the conversation, but from where I stood, I could see Mom shake—her hand, her voice, everything. "Uh-huh." She nodded. "I see."

Dr. Parker rattled on in her infomercial voice like everything was hunky-dory. "I'm certain that it's simply a reflex reaction at this point, Mrs. Jones, but I just wanted you to know." Know what? I wanted to scream it into the phone, but I kept my yap shut.

"Should we come down?" Mom sounded so lost.

"No, no. It was merely a reflex muscle twinge. I just wanted to keep you informed. But it is a good sign. Dr. Fields comes in from Rochester this evening. He can give us a better idea of how things are progressing."

"Good sign." Mom was losing it.

"Are you all right, Mrs. Jones?"

"Yes, thank you. Thank you so much."

Mom hung up right in the middle of Dr. Parker's good-bye.

"He moved!" I shouted, running into the kitchen.

Mom stood in the middle of the room, staring into the air. "This is not possible."

Clenching my fists, I begged Dad to show her just how possible it was, but nothing happened.

"Not possible, it's not," Mom mumbled her way into the living room. Stopping, she spun around, saying, "Dr. Ventro will have some answers."

"Ventro? You said he's a benzildug."

"He's a trained professional, Ebon. He knows what he's doing."

"What does he know about ghosts?"

"Don't argue with me, Ebon."

Benzildug or no benzildug, Mom would let Ventro into our house.

Dad's Back!
(Sort Of)

Sitting on my bed, I watched Fred case the molding under the cupboards looking for bugs. I could hear Samuel and Joliet milling around downstairs, calling for Dad, opening doors and drawers and shower curtains in search of him.

"Why'd you book it out of here like that, Ebon?" Dad's voice drifted into the room.

"Dad!"

"Shh!" Dad's finger materialized out of nowhere—right in front of my lips, but I felt nothing. I brought my hand up and it went through Dad's. He drew it back and giggled. *"That tickles!"*

"How?"

Dad moved his eyes to the far right, then to the far left, as if he were trying to get a look inside his head and find an answer. *"Haven't a clue."* In his housecoat again, he twirled the belt, saying, *"I started out in a dream version of our house. This place went on forever. Then I sort of drifted through Hamilton Hall into this maze of glassed-in shelves filled with books that have obscure facts hiding inside. I think I heard you scream. Next thing I know, I'm hungry for pickles. I go to the fridge and I can't grip the handle. It's like the handle turns to humid air or my hand does."* He stared at his hand, then shook his head. *"Either way, I can't open a thing, then you walk in and freak out."*

"What about the other night?"

"Well, I was working on a project and got stuck, so I did my rounds—checked on you kids. I went back to my desk and you showed up. I tried to help you out, and you went running and screaming like I was the grim reaper's supervisor. What's up?"

My heart turned inside out. Dad had no idea what was going on. "Dad, what . . . what time do you think it is now?"

He looked at his wrist—there was no watch. He checked the clock next to my bed. *"One o'clock? But I was just dreaming. But it's light out."* He stared out the window. He put his hand to his forehead as if to check his temperature. *"Am I sick? I can remember seeing you guys up on Picnic Glade. Why didn't you wait for me?"* He put his hands on his hips. *"And am I wacky, or did I see people in Hamilton Hall a while ago? Are you guys selling advance tickets or something?"*

"Dad, you're . . . you're not here."

"What?"

"You're not really here."

Dad smiled. *"Oh, I'm a figment of your imagination. That's good. Dad's a little loopy with a fever, and you decide to play a practical joke. How nice. Hitchcock would be intrigued. What's next?"*

"This isn't a joke." I jumped off the bed and went to the bathroom to open the door and turn on the light. "Look in the mirror."

Dad tried to do it, but nothing showed up. He stood there teetering, then he closed his eyes and backed up, chanting, *"Get a grip. Get a grip."* Passing through my bed and stumbling into a corner, Dad looked at me and said, *"Am I dead?"*

"No."

He held out his arms and looked at his hands. *"You can see through me, Ebon! I'm H. G. Wells's worst nightmare."*

"I'll go get Mom." I ran for the stairs.

"Wait!" Dad stood over me as I stopped on the first landing. *"Is that where you went last time?"*

"Yes."

"I saw all of you huddling together on the hill. I tried to open the door to yell out to you. I reached for the doorknob, and the next thing I know, I'm standing up here in my pj's."

"Everybody could see you from the hill."

"So I must fade away and come back, but why?"

"You're still here now."

Dad walked around to imitate his path as he said, *"When you ran away from me the other night, I tried to follow you, but when I went to go downstairs, I showed up in your room. You were all bundled up under your covers, and I went to you, but I never made it to the bed. What is going on here?"*

"I'll go get Mom." I ran downstairs. The back stairs in our house were designed by a modern-day Daedalus. All narrow and steep, you'd have to run down one flight, go out the door, then go in another door to go down the next flight. It was an aerobic workout extraordinaire. I was beat by the time I made it to the kitchen.

"Dr. Ventro will be here in a few minutes," Mom said as I stood in the doorway, leaning on my knees and trying to catch my breath.

"Who's he?" Dad appeared next to me and pulled his housecoat closed.

"Dad." I stood up and pointed.

Mom turned around. Dad waved.

"Is he here? I don't see a thing." Mom squinted to get a better look.

Dad waved even harder, saying, *"Yoo-hoo, right here."*

My mind started to buzz. Why couldn't she see him? Everyone had seen him from the hill when we huddled together. But no one else except me saw him around the house or even heard him.

I leaped forward and grabbed Mom's arm. Everyone on the hill had been touching me, so I figured touching her would make it possible for her to see Dad. She jumped at the shock of my sudden move, then she screamed and jumped again. It was like trying to hold on to a leaping frog, but from the open-mouthed stare on her face I knew she could see Dad.

"Luke."

"Let go, Ebon."

Dad caught on fast. I did as he told me to.

"He's gone," Mom shouted. Grabbing me, she smiled, saying, "There's my guy."

"You're a psychic antenna, Ebon!"

Just the thing I was hoping to become. But I would've gladly become a lamppost if it meant having Dad around again.

Mom staggered. I thought she'd fall over. "Hey, sweetie."

They stared at each other, each of them looking like they might cry. Then Dad blinked, saying, *"What happened, Wynne?"*

I felt like I should leave, but I couldn't. Standing between them made me feel the pull of their sadness. I began to wish I could disappear.

"You're . . . you're . . ."

"Please tell me I'm not dead."

"You're in a coma," Mom mumbled.

"A coma?"

"Is it really you?" She raised her hand in the air to touch Dad but let it drop onto my shoulder instead.

"As far as I know."

"How?"

The doorbell rang before Dad could answer.

"I'll get it." Dad was always happy to run for the door or the phone when he didn't want to face a tough question— Where do babies come from? Do grandparents have sex? Why was he see-through?

Mom usually yelled at him when he walked away from such questions, but this time she ran after him, dragging me along. Jumping in front of Dad, she yelled, "Don't open that door, Luke."

"Who's on the other side?"

"It's not him I'm worried about."

"Then what's the problem?" Dad reached for the door-knob; his hand went right through. *"Oh, that's a bit of a hurdle."*

Mom took a deep breath. "Luke, go in the piano room. I'll get rid of Dr. Ventro."

Dad backed into the grown-up lounge (our handle for the piano room). *"Ventro? What kind of name is that?"* He repeated the name real deep and long, as if announcing a superhero to a radio audience, *"Ventro!"*

"Luke," Mom growled in warning. She grabbed the doorknob as Samuel appeared on the landing of the main stairs.

"Is Dad here?" He ran into the foyer and started scanning around as if he'd just set off on an Easter egg hunt.

"Yeah." I grabbed Samuel by the shoulder as soon as he came into reach.

Squealing, he ran for Dad. "Where'd he go?"

I let go of Mom and caught up to Samuel. Seeing Dad again, Samuel thrust out his arms in tickling mode. Dad squeaked in laughter as Samuel tried to hug and touch him, but Samuel slipped right through Dad. Holding on to a wet fish had to be easier than keeping up with Samuel.

Joliet ran in, all smiles and tears, asking, "Where is he? I can hear him."

"Grab Ebon!" Samuel shouted as Mom watched in awe.

Dr. Ventro pounded on the door. "Is everything okay in there?"

"Just a minute," Mom called.

"Hi, Jolie." Dad smiled at her.

Joliet held my hand as she stared at Dad.

Samuel tried to touch Dad again. Confused, he said, "Whoa, you're like smoke."

Dad stood between Joliet and the couch trying to decide what to do. Mom looked from Dad to the door, struggling to do the same. I just wanted to melt.

Dr. Ventro pounded again. "Wynne? I'm sorry. Mrs. Jones?"

"Go away!" I shouted.

"Ebon! Ebon, is that you?" Dr. Ventro yelled.

"Dr. Ventro," Mom spoke through the door, "I can handle this. I'll call tomorrow."

"Are you sure?"

"The children don't want to see you now," Mom explained.

Dr. Ventro tried to peek in the window, so I stood in front of it and shouted, "Go away!"

"I can help, Ebon."

Who is this guy? Dad stood behind me, his jaw stiff, his eyes squinted in anger.

Mom grabbed my shoulder, then shook her other hand like she was trying to scare away a bee. "Go on, Luke. He'll see you."

Dad waved his hand in front of Dr. Ventro's face as he babbled on about talking out your problems with an outsider. He didn't even blink.

"He can't see me, Wynne. Who is he?"

"A psychologist."

"We need a parapsychologist a little more, but I think you should let him in."

"And tell him what?" Mom asked.

"Mrs. Jones." Dr. Ventro knocked again. "I really think we should talk."

"The kids are in trouble, Wynne. We're in trouble."

"And what's he going to do about it?"

"Let him in and we'll find out."

Mom opened the door. Dr. Ventro looked around as if he thought bats might come flying out, then stepped inside. As soon as he put his foot on our ivy-bordered welcome mat, Dad disappeared. I would've screamed, but Samuel was doing enough of that already.

The Big Questions

"Tell me what I can do to help," said Dr. Ventro, or Vento, as we liked to call him.

Mom pointed at the stairs. "You can go upstairs to the first room on the right-hand side while I calm my children down."

I loved how Mom talked to Vento as if he were a kindergartner in search of the bathroom. Samuel and Joliet didn't notice. Samuel had started to cry, and Joliet made a charge for the stairs. Mom grabbed her arm, saying, "Stay here."

"I don't want to talk to that drip."

"I can help you, Joliet," Vento said from the doormat. He still hadn't moved.

"You can go upstairs to my husband's study," Mom said to him. If the air hadn't been so heavy with all those grimy emotions—sadness, anger, and fear—I would've laughed at the way Mom treated old drippy-head Vento. What made things even better was the fact that he did as she told him and marched right up the stairs.

Joliet pulled away from Mom and tried to go upstairs, but Mom jumped up two steps to get in front of her. "We have to talk about this, Jolie."

"Then why's he here? Can't we talk about it as a family? You brought that creep in here and Dad disappeared."

As plain as if she were ordering a cup of coffee at McDonald's, Mom said, "Your father was never here."

"What?" I shouted.

"He wasn't here." Mom walked back downstairs and went into the grown-up lounge. We all followed her, shouting protests.

I screamed, "How can you say that? You saw him. We all did."

Mom turned. We circled around her. She held out her hands as if to keep us back, saying, "I won't deny that, but he wasn't really here. We just saw what we wanted to see."

Everyone spoke at once. It was like a gym class of kids fighting for the best ball. Joliet insisted she could see the birthmark on the back of Dad's hand. Samuel smelled cucumbers. I didn't need to remember any details. I could feel it inside. Dad had come home.

"Calm down!" Mom shouted. "We all want your father back so much we're seeing things."

"All of us?" I asked.

"At the same time?" Joliet added.

"Yes." Mom nodded. "Think of the people in churches who see tears of blood on a crucifix or the image of the Virgin Mary weeping on a hillside. They're group hallucinations."

"What?" Samuel asked.

"We imagined him, honey." Mom rubbed Samuel's back and tried to give him a hug, but Samuel pulled away.

"He was here!" Samuel shouted.

"Then where is he now?" Mom asked. Everyone started to look around.

I couldn't understand why Mom didn't believe in Dad's spirit. He'd stood right in front of her. She'd talked to him. She'd even yelled at him. I tried to find the moment she stopped believing what she saw. When I recalled the expression on her face as she opened the door, I knew it happened when Dr. Ventro appeared. Dad disappeared in an instant when Vento the Ventilated came in.

I wanted to know where Dad had gone. I swore that if Dad didn't come back, I'd dump a box of tacks in Vento's bed and make him sleep on them for the rest of his life.

"You're wrong, Mom," Joliet said, shaking her head.

"All right, Joliet. How did he get here? What was he?"

Samuel shouted, "He was here. He was real!" He started to cry again.

Hugging Samuel, Mom said, "This is too crazy."

In my head I begged Dad to show up. Just for an instant. Dad'd know what to do. He'd do the right thing.

Mom pulled away, saying, "I'm sorry to leave you, but I need to talk to Dr. Ventro for just a minute. I'll be right back." She headed for the stairs.

Samuel shouted, "Dad will too!" He turned to me after Mom left and said, "He'll be back."

I nodded, but part of me didn't believe him. I went to the stairs and watched Mom go into the study. What if Dad came back because we wanted him to? What if we all had to believe in order for him to show up? Did Mom make him disappear for good?

I went to the door of the study to listen in. I could hear Mom crying. Dr. Ventro's voice sounded garbled and blubbery. I pressed against the door.

"Ebon, that's rude." Dad's voice came from behind me.

I jumped, knocking my head on the doorknob. Turning, I saw Dad standing barefoot in the hallway wearing a pair of khaki shorts and a polo shirt. A pair of sunglasses hung out of his pocket.

"Where'd you go?"

Dad looked at himself. Grabbing the sunglasses, he held them up, saying, *"The beach? I have no clue."*

"What's happening, Dad?"

"Same verdict for that question." He pointed at the door. *"Your mother in there with the psychologist?"*

"She thinks you're a hallucination."

Dad smiled. *"You said that perfectly. You've been practicing."*

"Dad." I hated it when he went goofy at a really serious moment.

"I'm sorry." He turned to the stairs. *"Where are Joliet and Samuel?"*

"Downstairs."

"*Go down and get them. I'll be in the Shroom Forest.*" Dad went to the back stairs, and I headed down to collect everyone else. When I told them I'd seen Dad, they just about ran me over to get upstairs. I raced past them. On the landing I said in the lowest, meanest voice possible, "Be quiet, or Mom and Ventro will come out!"

They obeyed me, and we all snuck up to the Shroom Forest. Dad stood in the doorway of Samuel's bedroom staring. Holding one another's hands, we waited for him to speak.

"*Samuel,*" he said the name in a whisper.

"Yes, Dad."

"*Come here.*" Dad stepped inside, his face droopy and sad.

Joliet and I followed Samuel in. We all dragged our feet, afraid of what Dad would say. I stepped into the room and stopped. I knew what had made Dad so glum.

The bed had been made, the bedspread smoothed flat. The only things touching the floor were the feet of the furniture. The dresser drawers had been pushed in, with no clothes hanging out, the walls stripped bare.

"*What happened to your room?*" Dad asked.

"I wanted you to come home," Samuel said. He put his free hand up to grab Dad's, but it went right through.

Dad cried. He slumped down, went through the bed, and ended up on the floor. "*Oh, kids. I'm so sorry.*"

"Don't cry, Daddy." Samuel crouched down to look Dad in the face. "I like it clean."

"*No, you don't.*" Dad shook his head and smiled. "*You love your mess.*"

"I love you, Dad," Samuel said. "I wanted to show God we could be good, so he'd send you back to us."

Dad jumped to his feet. "*You weren't bad, Samuel.*"

Samuel's comment made me cringe inside. Was that why Dad had come back? We'd prayed and God had given us what we wanted, but what if Dad was really supposed to go to heaven? That thought was too heavy to keep in my head, so I moved on. What if taking Dad from his body made his body die? What if he wasn't able to get back to his body again? It would be miserable if we could never touch him.

"Dad." Joliet stood by the dresser, picking at the varnish. "Mom thinks we're making you up."

"*I'm real, Joliet. Real enough to have my own thoughts.*" He touched his face. "*But not real enough to feel my own tears.*"

"Are you a ghost?" Samuel asked.

"*I don't know.*"

"Ghosts are of dead people," I pointed out.

"You're not dead, are you?" Samuel asked.

"He isn't!" I shouted in reflex.

Dad started to pace. "*There's got to be a reason for all this.*"

I tried to think of a reason, but my brain cramped.

"You went to heaven by mistake, but God sent you back because you weren't dead yet," Samuel suggested.

Dad hummed. "*I can't remember any bright lights or pearly gates, so I don't think that's it.*"

"You're an angel!" Samuel shouted.

We all laughed.

"Not a chance!" Joliet yelled. Dad looked at her, eyebrows raised. She giggled. "Sorry, Dad."

For that tiny instant, when we laughed, Dad was real. Real in the sense that I forgot he was see-through. I didn't think of the body sleeping in a hospital bed. He was there with us and we felt happy.

Dr. Vento, the Demented

The happiness didn't last. Mom called us into the study. Dad said we had to go. Still linked, we kids walked in and slumped down together into Dad's love seat. He followed us to the door, but Vento-Bento-Dento-brain closed it in Dad's face. I sat on the couch waiting for Dad to walk through the door, but he didn't.

"Children." Dr. Ventro sat in Dad's chair, his hands together in a steeple. He was the first person I'd ever seen whose feet didn't dangle in the air when he sat in Dad's chair—his Speedster, as Dad called it. I wanted to stick my foot out and push the chair so it would tip back and spill him onto the window seat.

The only problem was Mom sat in the window seat behind him. I was also mad at her for doubting Dad and dragging Vento-Dento into the picture, but not mad enough to dump him on her.

"Children," he started over as if he'd never said a word. "Your mother tells me you saw an image of your father. Tell me about it."

Samuel stood up to say, "He was here. And you can't change that."

"All right." Ventro nodded. "Anyone else?"

I didn't speak because I knew his game. He was going to twist our words around until we didn't believe ourselves, and Dad would disappear. I became convinced that Dad had come back because we wanted him to and we believed he could. I thought he'd disappear if we stopped believing.

Joliet probably agreed with me, because she kept silent as well. To keep my mind off Ventro and his spitty lips, I stared at the mirror across the room. I could see all of us kids scrunched together on the couch—elbows in one another's armpits, legs tangled up—a human rope all tied together. We could keep Dad with us. He'd stay forever.

"Kids." Having Ventro look at us made me shiver, but he just kept right on talking. "When you become ill, your mind can play tricks on you and make things appear that aren't really there."

"I saw a tiger come through the wall and jump into the wastebasket when I had mono," Samuel said, sounding like he was back in second-grade show-and-tell.

"Yes, that's a good example, Samuel."

Way to help the drip out, I thought.

Ventro smiled, and I wanted to grab the stapler by his elbow and pinch his lips together with it, but he babbled along. "Has anyone else had that happen?"

No one spoke. I imagined a little scoreboard on the far wall that read in bright lights, VENTRO 1, JONES 0.

"Well, sadness can be a sickness too, and it makes you see things that aren't there."

"Oh, I know, it happens to me all the time." Dad appeared, leaning against the wall in his long painting coat, cutoffs, and a T-shirt as speckled with paint as his coat.

We kids giggled. We knew enough not to give Dad away, but we couldn't keep from laughing. I looked to Mom; she didn't move. She just stared at Dr. Ventro and hugged her knees.

"Do you understand?" Ventro asked.

I wanted to say, "No, I don't understand how my mom can say my dad isn't really right here. There he is. Look at him!"

"Oh, I understand perfectly, Doctor. It's as clear as black paint on a chalkboard." Dad nodded.

The other kids laughed, but I had my eyes on Mom. She stared at the floor and began to rock. *She can really hear him,* I told myself. The trouble was she didn't want to; but why?

"Hey"—Dad stepped up to the desk—*"this guy wears a toupee."*

Joliet bent forward in laughter.

"What's a toupee?" Samuel asked.

Dr. Ventro grabbed the top of his head, saying, "Excuse me?"

Mom burst out laughing right along with the rest of us. The room was so full of laughter we could've floated like the guy in *Mary Poppins.*

Dr. Ventro looked like he had ketchup seeping out of his

pores, he was so red. "I fail to see the humor in all of this."

"I'm sure you would." Dad leaned on the desk next to Ventro. They were just inches from each other. *"But that's only because you can't see me, Baldy."*

Looking at us, Mom whispered, "It's your dad, isn't it?" We all nodded, choking on laughter. By this time it had to be Ventro 1 and Jones 50, thanks to Dad.

"Oh." Dr. Ventro nodded. "You can hear your husband, Mrs. Jones? Is he here now?"

"Yep." Dad stood up. *"Watch this."* He stepped over to his computer. *"I know I can do this one."* He flicked the power switch. Hearing the snap of the switch gave my heart a jump start. Dad had touched something and actually made it move! Was his body coming to join him? Or was he going to be a solid-type ghost that could play tricks on people, closing doors and turning off lights?

All the parts of Dad's computer were connected, so the printer next to Vento-Pimento came on with a growl. He wiggled out of the chair in a fright. I'd never seen a guy slither like a snake before.

"Luke!" Mom shouted.

"So, I am here, then?" Dad leaned toward Mom, smiling.

"The question is, should you be?" Mom had actually heard Dad! She stood up, staring at where she figured he stood.

"Now, Wynne." Ventro held up a hand. "It's not good to indulge in this fantasy. For the sake of the children—"

Mom and Dad turned together to shout, *"Stuff it!"*

We kids squirmed and giggled on the couch like a pile of worms. I'd pay a million dollars for a videotape of that time in the office. Dad tormenting old Vento. Mom and Dad working together as if Dad had never fallen asleep. The three of us kids laughing until we came close to watering the couch.

"Now, Wynne." Vento the Demento said it like he'd caught Mom cheating on a test.

"That's Mrs. Jones." Mom walked forward, backing Ventro toward the door. "And I think this is something we'll have to work out ourselves."

She opened the door for him. He backed out, shouting, "It's unhealthy to participate in group hallucinations."

"Good riddance," Dad said as Mom slammed the door.

We kids gasped for air as Mom said, "Go upstairs, kids, your father and I need to talk."

We all melted into silence and watched Dad. He stared at Mom with his I-love-you-and-I'm-so-sorry-things-aren't-flying-smoothly look.

"You can't even see him without me here," I said.

"I don't need to see him to talk, Ebon."

I got up first, with a full-fledged plan to listen through the heat vent in Samuel's bathroom.

A Little Bit
of Heaven

I reached Samuel's bathroom first. We all crowded around the old iron grate in the floor. We could even see into the room below. Dad's pale face looked up at us. *"Sorry, guys, we're going to Castle Rook. No visitors allowed."*

After a group moan of disappointment, we ran to the hall window so we could see Castle Rook. Mom crossed the yard. Dad, faint like fog, floated behind her. The sun bleached him white.

"Eerie," Joliet whispered. "What do you think is happening to his body when he does that?"

"I don't know," I said.

"How can you have a ghost of a living person?" Joliet wasn't really talking to us, she just asked.

"Pastor Crebber says ghosts are evil," Samuel added.

"Cut it out." Joliet pushed Samuel. "Dad's not evil."

"I didn't say he was."

"Just be quiet." I held up my hands. Mom came out the back door of Castle Rook. "Look." I pointed. We waited; Dad didn't emerge.

"She made him go away," Samuel gasped.

"No, she didn't." Joliet swatted him.

We listened as Mom walked up the back steps. As she

reached the landing we could see Dad behind her. "Let's all go into Shroom Forest," Mom said, leading the way.

Everyone settled into our shrooms except for Dad, who sort of hovered in the corner behind Mom. Our feet mingled in the center of the shroom circle, so everyone could see him.

Mom took a deep breath, then said, "Joliet, you were right. We should talk about this as a family."

Dad crouched down to say, "*We have to figure this out.*" He spoke right next to Mom's ear. She closed her eyes to listen. I did too. His voice sounded whole and solid. I imagined him sitting in the double shroom with Mom.

"*I'll tell you what I know. I remember going to bed that night. Your mom and I talked about fruit bats and how to sculpt bat wings. I fell asleep in there somewhere.*"

"While I was telling you about my conversation with the boys' teacher," Mom laughed, but I could tell she was still a little annoyed.

"*I remember.*" Dad nodded, squinting over the memory. "*I had a dream—one of those searching-for-knowledge, your-own-house-suddenly-has-extra-rooms kinds of dreams. I walked through the halls of our house to tuck everyone in, but the rooms had all been stretched. You kids slept a mile from your doorways. I tried to walk to Joliet's bed. I ended up in Hamilton Hall instead. I turned to leave, but I couldn't remember the way out. When I started to hunt for my guidebook, the whole place filled up with bookshelves, until it looked like I'd wandered into the Library of Congress. I couldn't even find the end of a row.*"

An endless library? Now, that had to be Dad's idea of heaven. But a maze? I'd hate to be stuck in any kind of maze.

Dad went on. *"I felt pulled in. I wanted to read the books, but not without you kids. I just couldn't find you. The next thing I know, I'm standing at the top of the stairs in Ebon's room and he screams."*

"Why'd you have to scream?" Joliet pushed me. I had to open my eyes.

Dad put out his hand. *"Don't be hard on each other. This isn't anybody's fault."*

There was a pounding from below. Samuel jumped, asking, "What's that?"

"It's just someone at the door, Samuel," Dad said.

Leaning to block our exit, Joliet said, "Don't answer it."

"Why not?" Mom asked.

"Any time an outsider comes in, Dad disappears."

"Good point." I nodded. The pounding got louder. Whoever it was really wanted our attention.

"We have to answer it." Mom stood up, but Samuel hugged her tight to keep her from going. Joliet and I tried to block her.

"All right, I'll answer it." Dad went for the back stairs. We raced down the front.

Dad beat us. He stood at the door, smiling. *"Hey, this has some perks."* He closed his eyes to concentrate, but he still couldn't grip the door.

"Let me, Luke." Mom leaned forward and opened it.

A lady in a blue raincoat stood on the steps. It'd started to rain, so she was all hunched over and wet. "Mrs. Jones," she said. Mom rushed her into the house as she continued, "Dr. Parker sent me. We've been trying to call, but your phone's been busy."

It hit me like a flash flood. I'd left the phone off the hook when Dr. Parker called earlier.

"What is it?" Mom asked.

"Dr. Parker wants you to come to the hospital."

"Why?" Mom started to shake. Dad looked scared too.

"Your husband's vital signs are weakening."

Weakening? But Dad was standing right beside us! He was doing great—laughing and talking and playing jokes on old Vento.

"Come on, kids," Mom herded us toward the hall closet. "Get your coats. We've got to go."

The lady stood right between Mom and Dad. I wanted to push her out the door. Mom searched for Dad but couldn't see him. He leaned toward her and whispered, *"Go."*

"I love you." Mom said it out loud, and the nurse blushed, then realized Mom was looking at someone behind her. She turned, and *poof,* Dad vanished.

We screamed, but it did no good. He was gone. We ran for the car.

At the hospital Mom tried to leave us in the waiting room, but we all followed her to the nurses' station. Leaning over the counter, she asked, "Dr. Parker?"

"She's with your husband, Mrs. Jones."

Before the nurse could stop us, we all went into Dad's room. Dr. Parker looked like she'd just tucked him in. When she saw us coming, she came forward, putting up her arms like a blockade. "It's okay. It's okay." Backing us into the hall, she said, "His vital signs dipped a little, but he just stabilized."

"Just now?" Mom asked.

"In the last fifteen minutes or so."

I knew what Mom had in mind. I thought it too. It had taken us fifteen minutes to drive to the hospital. Dad had disappeared fifteen minutes ago. Coming back to the house was ruining Dad's chances of coming home. Guilt coated my insides like boiled milk sticking to the side of a pan.

We went to the waiting room. Mom didn't want to leave until she was sure Dad had stabilized. I didn't want her to go anywhere. I held her tight. Joliet hugged me, and Samuel slid in under Mom's other arm. I didn't want to think about Dad, because I knew it'd make him come around. It was all my fault. I kept bringing him back with all my stupid questions.

"Is Dad going to die?" Samuel asked.

Silent for a moment, Mom said, "I don't know, honey."

"Don't say that," I said.

"Oh, Ebon." Mom rubbed my head. "Your father loves us so much he can't let go. We keep pulling him back."

I sat up, asking, "Do you think he was supposed to die?"

"That's just it, Ebon. I don't know." Mom hugged me so hard it hurt a little.

If she didn't know, who did?

Just then, some guy with a halo of red bristles for hair came into the waiting room. "Mrs. Jones?"

"Yes?" Mom answered.

The man, who seemed to be carrying a balloon under his shirt, sat down beside her, saying, "I'm Dr. Fields."

"The neurologist from Rochester?"

"That's right." When he smiled, I saw that gold lined one of his teeth. "I have some news to share with you."

"Good news?" I asked.

"Well . . ." He looked at his shoes. We'd just met him, and already he had bad news to tell us. "Let's just say it's mixed. Would you like to come into the consolation room?"

"No." Mom shook her head. "The children can hear."

"We've found the problem."

Mom held on tighter. I felt stiff all over. "What is it?" Mom asked.

"It's a micro tear at the base of the brain."

A tear? As in a rip? In the brain? This was the worst possible news.

"Now, what that means is that the injury was severe enough to push him into a coma, but it doesn't mean it's not repairable."

"He'll need surgery?"

Dr. Fields looked down again. "No, ma'am. Surgery isn't an option. We have no way to fuse the tear ourselves, but the brain is an amazing organ. It often compensates for injuries by rerouting information. Once it has time to recover from the shock of this injury, your husband's brain may reactivate itself."

Rerouting? Was that it? Dad had found a new route through his brain that allowed him to separate into two people? Now we just had to help him find the way back to his body. But would his body ever be okay?

"How likely is it that he'll recover?" Mom asked.

"I'd say a fifty-fifty chance that he'll regain consciousness. But be aware that there may be some residual damage."

Mom nodded. Dr. Fields asked if we had any more questions. I wanted to know if he always talked about someone's odds as if living or dying depended on the flip of a coin, but Mom thanked him and he went away.

Putting her arms around all three of us, she whispered, "We need to pray, kids."

I asked God to turn the coin in our favor, but it felt more like I'd turned in a request for a miracle. That could be one tall order.

The Answer
Man

Dad usually claimed the title the Answer Man. He considered it a personal challenge when someone asked him a question he didn't know the answer to, like where exactly is Timbuktu, anyway? He'd hunt and scrounge until he found it. (It's a city in northwestern Africa, by the way, Mali to be exact.) Any time I had a question that made me feel the least bit empty, I'd go to Dad, he'd find the answer, and just like that, I'd feel fuller.

Knowing why Dad had gone into a coma didn't help. It didn't even matter how it happened. What I had to know was how Dad could be in two places at once. And what could make him healthy and whole. Where could I go to find a way to make that happen?

The last place I wanted to go was to school, especially after spending the night in the hospital waiting room. The next morning Dad still slept like a princess entranced by a witch (why didn't that ever happen to a prince, anyway?). Since we could do nothing more at the hospital, Mom sent us all to school. She'd fallen back into her "act normal" routine.

When we dropped Joliet off at her school, Mom got out to have a talk with her. I didn't dare roll down my window to eavesdrop. Joliet stomped off. Whatever Mom said, it wasn't good.

Samuel and I got her little speech at our school. Expecting it, we just sat there when she stopped the car.

"Boys," she sighed. "I think it'd be best if we didn't encourage your dad."

"Encourage him?" Samuel asked.

"To do what?" I added.

Mom looked down. "Everything your father does as a spirit affects his physical body, so we need to stop encouraging him to come back to the house."

"You want us to ignore him?" I asked. Mom had hatched another ugly scheme.

She nodded. "Yes."

"No way!" Samuel and I shouted together.

Mom turned to face both of us. "I know it'll be hard, but it's the best thing we can do for your father right now. We need to do what we can to put his two selves back together. Keeping him at home, away from his body, isn't doing him any good."

In a flash Mom had given me the answer. I had to get Dad's spirit to the hospital.

"Okay, Mom!" I yelled as I rushed out of the car and ran into the school in search of B. J. It was my turn to be the Answer Man, and B. J. was going to help me make it happen.

I found her in the library hunting for a book. B. J. jiggled when she saw me. All of her excitement flowed into her mouth as she spewed out words faster than my mom could chew through wood with her stonecutter. "Hey, Ebon, has your dad shown up again? I tried and tried calling. The line stayed busy for hours. My dad wouldn't let me come over. He said it was rude. He's rude."

"He's shown up, all right. Now we've got to get him back to his body."

"Excuse me?"

I pulled her out into the hall. "Let's talk on the move." Leaving school by our bathroom-window route, we headed through the park as I gave B. J. the scoop. "If we want Dad back, then we've got to get his spirit and his body back together."

As I ran I could hear, B. J. shout, "Oh."

We cut over to Nicollet Avenue to catch a bus back home. As we stopped on the corner to catch our breath B. J. asked, "How are you going to get him to show up?"

Major roadblock. I still had no idea how to get Dad to show up. There was no pattern to it. He'd popped in for a bite to eat. How could he be hungry? He'd made his nightly rounds. I didn't have that long to wait. He had appeared to taunt Vento the Demento, but would he do it again? What the heck, it was worth a spin.

Instead of taking the bus home, we took it straight to Ventro's office. His secretary was a short guy with hair that looked like an overused toothbrush, all stiff in one spot, then saggy in another. "Dr. Ventro will be with you in just a moment," he said as he hung up the phone.

I didn't feel like waiting a minute, but I had no choice. I should have known not to trust Bristle Head. It took Ventro a whole twenty minutes to get done talking to some kid with a Band-Aid over her left eye. He walked her to the elevator, then came to talk to me.

"Ebon, this sure is a surprise. Who have you brought with you?"

"Belinda Taggert." B. J. offered her hand. Ventro shook it. She scrunched up her face, so I knew she was giving him the B. J. death grip, but Ventro kept right on smiling.

"Come on into my office and tell me what's up."

We walked into his little romper room. When he closed the door, I said, "I just wanted to use your office for a bit."

"My office?"

"Yeah, I need to find my dad so I can take him to the hospital."

Ventro looked confused; he bunched up his eyebrows. "Is your father lost, Ebon?"

"I guess you could say that." I walked behind Ventro's desk and messed with his Rolodex. All the while I thought, *Come on Dad, show up.*

"How'd he get lost, Ebon?"

Knowing the truth wouldn't sink in with Ventro, I used it as a stalling tactic. I figured it'd give his analytical mind a spin. "You know, he fell into a coma, then his spirit showed up at our house. I'm just trying to get his body and his spirit in one place."

"I see." He nodded, one of those adult-pretending-to-understand nods, then asked, "And how do you plan to do that?"

Listening to Ventro's stupid questions, I knew exactly why they were called head shrinkers. They clouded your mind with questions until it's too crowded to think straight, then you had to let everything out of your mind to clear the thought jam. That just left you with an empty head. I couldn't take it anymore. I shouted, "Dad? Where are you?"

Nothing.

B. J. stared at the rug, and Ventro got all sad eyed. Typical Dad. When I needed him the most, he was nowhere in sight. The whole thing made me mad enough to rearrange Ventro's furniture a little—an overturned chair, couch cushions across the room, ugly alphabet rug kicked into a heap. It looked pretty good by the time I'd finished.

B. J. yelled at me to stop, and Ventro told me to "let it all out." I wanted to let him out. Shove him right out the door and never let him back in. I went for a painting on the wall. I saw myself smashing it over a chair, the glass popping into the air like fireworks.

"*Ebon!*" Dad's voice boomed right through me. It felt like it came from inside me. I froze. Dad stood next to me, his face in a gargoyle-style frown. *"Slow the train down, son. Talk to me."*

"Where were you? Why didn't you show up when I called?"

Dr. Ventro grabbed me by the shoulders, saying, "Ebon, you've lost control. There's no one here but us. Just you, me, and Belinda."

"Leave my son alone!" Dad yelled right in Vento the Demento's ear, but it had no effect. The drip didn't even flinch.

Ventro tried to steer me to the couch. I begged, "Do something, Dad!"

Dad ran across the room. He passed through B. J. and she jumped as if she'd touched a hot stove.

"See!" I shouted, pointing to B. J. She'd felt him.

Ventro turned to look at B. J. just as Dad turned on the floor lamp beside the couch. Ventro got a full blast of light torture. He screamed. Covering his eyes, he teetered a little.

"All right, Dad!" I shouted.

B. J. rubbed her arms, saying, "I did feel him. I did!"

"Come on, Dad." I jumped up and ran for the door. "Let's go!"

B. J. followed right behind me, but I wasn't sure Dad had stayed with us until we got into the elevator. He looked faint in the fluorescent lights, but he stood there—in jeans and the green sweatshirt he'd gotten for coaching Samuel's team through the shortest Little League season in history. They had a blast, but they couldn't play baseball worth diddly.

"Is he here with us?" B. J. asked.

Dad leaned in close to B. J.'s ear, then said, *"Belinda Jane the Toffee Brain."* Dad called her that because she had eaten enough toffee one Christmas to sugarcoat her brain.

She giggled. "I heard him."

"Really?" I asked.

"Hey, I'm getting better at this." Dad stood up, smiling.

"Maybe that's not such a good idea, Dad."

"Where is he?" B. J. squinted to try to see him.

"Why not?" Dad asked me.

I couldn't look at Dad, but I managed to say, "Whenever you do something wild your body goes kind of wonky."

"Huh?"

B. J. pointed to where I was talking. "Is he right there?"

I nodded. B. J. stared in awe.

"Dad, if you don't get back to your body soon, bad things could happen."

"Worse than not being able to eat, sleep, or hug my kids? Not likely."

"It could happen, Dad." I wanted to cry.

Dad leaned over so we were face-to-face. I could feel the warmth of him on my cheeks, like static on a blanket when you first take it out of the dryer. He said, *"I'm sorry, buddy."*

"It's not your fault."

"Not just about this whole mess." He waved his hands in the air; his right hand swung over B. J.

"I felt that." B. J. grabbed her head.

"I'm sorry I didn't hear you at first, Ebon."

Dad not hearing me was nothing new. He could research during a fire drill. He'd get into the zone, and the rest of the world would disappear. Last spring Samuel got his foot stuck in the storm drain in front of the house. We called for Dad with enough volume to bring Mr. Taggert out of his house a hundred yards away, but Dad didn't hear a thing. He looked completely surprised when Mr. Taggert carried Samuel upstairs.

Part of me wanted to make Dad feel better and tell him it was okay, but I also wanted him to know how sorry he should feel for disappearing into his work all of the time. Maybe it was his fault after all. His black-hole research binges had led to a permanent disease.

No, that was stupid. All that mattered was getting Dad back into his body.

"We need to get you to the hospital, Dad."

"Good idea, sport." Dad smiled, but he still looked sad. *"I'll be a better listener, Ebon. I promise."*

"Thanks, Dad."

"When this is over, I'm going to settle in to a normal routine. I'll be an ordinary guy." Dad sounded like he was making a bargain with God. Sacrificing something to be brought back into his body.

Could Dad actually be an ordinary guy? He couldn't even mow the lawn in straight lines. He always mowed shapes and left the rest of it long to show off his new creation. Last Halloween he mowed a pumpkin into our lawn, then spray-painted it orange. People drove by our house at all hours to look at that stupid pumpkin. Some guy from the *Tribune* even came by to take a picture and interview Dad about Hamilton Hall. Dad could never be just an ordinary guy, but I couldn't help thinking that he might have the right idea with his promise to be normal. This kind of stuff never happened to an ordinary guy.

Ebon's Plan
in Action

We hopped on a bus to get to the hospital, but nobody gave Dad any room. When I picked a seat and sat on the edge to give Dad a little space, some guy got on with a pile of books and looked down at me like I was a Boy Scouts reject. I stood up to let him sit down, and he slid right through Dad. I could see Dad's head and shoulders coming out of the guy's hat.

The guy started shifting and shrugging. He felt Dad. "Come on," I said, waving at Dad to stand up with me. The guy gave me a crazy look, but Dad stood up.

Rubbing his stomach, Dad said, *"You know what? When that guy slid into me, I could taste liver and onions. I think he had liver and onions for lunch. Too bad he didn't have dessert."*

"Weird," B. J. said.

"You heard that?" I asked.

"Sure."

"Can you see him?"

Dad leaned real close to B. J. and made a fish face. I laughed, but B. J. just blinked. "Nope."

I didn't want to tell her about the psychic antenna feature of my personality. I guess part of me still wanted someone to see Dad without me poking in.

"Hey, don't worry, Ebon. It'll all work out." Dad put his hand up to pat me, then he stuck it into his pocket.

"And how do you know?"

"Okay, so I don't." Just as Dad said that, some lady with a handful of shopping bags stood right where Dad was. He giggled and staggered backward. "Man, those bags tickle."

He stepped into a guy with an umbrella. Shivering, he squeezed into a space between a kid bobbing to his headphones and a lady reading the sports section. "That guy has a serious problem," Dad said, pointing at the umbrella man.

"What do you mean?" I leaned toward Dad, who was behind me by that point.

"He thinks they should pump mind-altering drugs through the air vents on city buses."

"How cruel." B. J. shook her head.

How weird. Dad could stand inside other human beings and hear their thoughts. This couldn't be a good sign for getting Dad back to normal. I had to get Dad to the hospital, and soon. More and more people crammed into the bus, until there was no place left for Dad to stand. I knew I couldn't stand being forced to listen to some stranger's thoughts. It'd be too much like being possessed by an evil spirit.

Stuck inside a lady with a stroller, Dad shouted, "I've got to get out of here!" He sidestepped right off the bus.

"Grab the cord!" I shouted at B. J. She jumped up and

pulled it. The bus jerked to a stop at the corner, but it took us forever to push our way through the crowd.

I kept checking the street for Dad. I didn't want him to disappear. When we hit the sidewalk, I felt positive that he would be gone, but there he sat, with his feet in the gutter and his head in his hands.

"Dad?"

"That woman was remembering the bath she gave her little kid this morning. You have any idea what it's like to bathe a baby?" He held his hands out. *"They're so small you can hold them in your hand."* I didn't remember ever seeing him with a baby, but I had seen him hide an entire orange in one palm. *"You're holding their life. Making little suds on their soft skin. Keeping the soap out of their eyes. They laugh when you slap the water."*

I should have said something, but a lady stood on the corner staring at us like we were Martians or something.

B. J. smiled. Dad smiled back, but she didn't see it. *"I want to feel things so badly my heart aches, but all I've got is air!"* He waved his arms in front of him, connecting with nothing.

"We've got to get Dad to the hospital," I said.

I didn't want to think anymore. I just wanted to do. I wanted to get Dad to the hospital and see him become a whole person again. With a bus ride out of the picture, we had a lot of ground to cover on foot before we could get to the hospital.

"I wonder where you go when you're not around?" B. J. asked as we got under way.

"I don't know, Belinda. I only remember the times when I'm with Wynne and the kids. It's like I'm stuck inside of a movie and I just flash from one scene to the next. There's nothing in between."

"Too much," B. J. said as we turned a corner.

We walked in silence for another block, then Dad stopped. I turned to face him. He wavered a little. He didn't stagger. He looked like a TV image that didn't come in clearly. His image had started to break up.

"Dad?"

"It doesn't make sense, but I'm tired." Dad yawned.

"Tired? How could you be tired?"

"I don't know."

"We better hurry, then." I started to run and so did B. J. Usually Dad would be half a block ahead, but he barely kept up. I didn't want to look at him anymore. I wanted to be at the stupid hospital.

"Just two more blocks, Dad!" I shouted.

"Okay," he gasped back.

All I could think to do was pray that Dad made it to the hospital. By the time we reached the front steps, Dad had actually started to pant. He leaned forward and gripped his knees. *"I don't think I can make it up those steps, Eb."*

"Let's go in through Emergency." I darted around the side of the building, Dad dragging himself behind me.

B. J. jumped on the electric mat to trigger the door, and we went in. I took an immediate left to get out of everyone's way. Dad wasn't much more than a wispy image of himself once we got to his ward. He was breathing so heavily he sounded like he was about to have an asthma attack.

"Hold on, Dad."

Bells started going off as we approached Dad's room and nurses went running. I heard someone shout, "Check his airway."

I ran to his room.

"You can't go in there." A nurse grabbed ahold of me to keep me from going in.

"I have to!" I shouted, trying to pull away, but she had me good. Dad kept right on walking. Dr. Parker stood over his solid body, listening to his chest through a stethoscope; a nurse checked Dad's throat. His body panted as hard as his spirit.

"Go, Dad, go," I whispered. The nurse tried to back B. J. and me toward the waiting room, but I slipped to the side and grabbed ahold of a food cart. She couldn't push me and the cart, so she had to pry my hands off. I held tight. I even thought of biting her, but I kept my eyes on Dad. He walked straight into the bed. I prayed he'd disappear into himself, but he didn't. He just stood over his own body and stared.

His shoulders started to tremble, and someone shouted, "His heart rate's rising."

No, don't make it worse, I thought, shouting, "Dad!" He turned, and in a flash he disappeared. Just like that.

Seeing him vanish again pulled all the strength right out of me. I collapsed like a tent, and the nurse had to carry me into the waiting room. I closed my eyes, hugged B. J., and prayed for a miracle.

Before I said amen, Mom showed up, out of breath and shaky. The nurse took her straight to Dad, but she came back in a flash.

Drawing me into her arms, she said, "Hey, baby. Dad's okay. Breathing easy now."

B. J. leaned against Mom's shoulder as I said, "We tried to bring him back—put his body and his spirit together, just like you said."

She kissed me on the forehead. "You tried, baby. You tried." Mom gave me a hug, but it didn't make me feel any better. I just felt limp and tired and useless. *Sorry, Dad.*

Coming
Home

A weak strain of Rip van Winkle disease spread through-out our family. As soon as we got home, everyone went off to sleep. I saw Samuel climb into Mom and Dad's bed as I walked through the second-floor hallway. He almost looked peaceful next to Mom, but it was too close to the place where Dad had fallen asleep for me. Praying Dad wouldn't sink further away from us, I crawled into the window seat in Dad's study. I fell asleep trying to imagine Dad sitting there with me, reading a book.

A sputter and whir woke me up. I'd slept alone in the room. No sound led the way as I reached the hallway. Then from the kitchen I heard, *Gug-gug-vhrrrrrrrrrrr.* I went down the back stairs, thinking maybe Mom was in her shop crafting a gargoyle, but instead she was cranking the ice-cream maker. *Gug-gug-vhrrrrrrrr*—she let the handle spin itself out.

Seeing me, she tapped the machine, saying, "Seems all wrong without Luke hanging over my shoulder waiting for the first spoonful."

Leaning into Mom felt like the best way to say, "I agree."

"Need a hug?"

I was all hugged out, so I shook my head.

A. LaFaye
130

"Well, Samuel's out back cleaning Castle Rook, and Joliet went with Mary Becker to their art lesson." Giving the ice cream one more crank, she said, "Ebon, I know you really want to help your dad; so do I. But cutting school, barging in on Dr. Ventro, and racing around with your dad—these things are a little over the edge, kiddo. God knows, I'm going a little nuts myself. Half the time I feel like I'm trapped inside Hamilton Hall. And I find myself talking to your father even though he's nowhere near within earshot. I guess I just don't know what to do with you, Ebon. I don't know how to help."

"I'll cool it, Mom. I promise."

Usually it was Dad Mom didn't know what to do with. She always said to him, "Luke, you're impossible." He sent her into panic after panic. She never knew when he'd show up for a parent-teacher conference or a piano recital. Every other day he turned the house upside down with a new project.

And the accidents didn't make for peaceful times either. On a camping trip a few years back Dad climbed a tree with our food to keep it away from bears. He got so into the tree climbing that he kept going up and up. Mom told him he'd climb so high there'd be nothing strong enough to hold him. He didn't listen until after he'd proved her right by stepping on a weak branch. He started to fall, striking almost every branch on his way down, before he grabbed on to a lower branch and broke his fall, and his arm. Mom had to use tent poles to set it.

Even the people in the neighborhood and at school were clueless. As Dad carted blocks into the backyard to make Castle Rook, Mr. Taggert had asked, "What're you doing with those, Luke? Rebuilding your basement?"

"What, and destroy my bumper crop of mushrooms?" Dad asked. Our real basement was wet enough to support fish.

Mr. Taggert didn't laugh. Dad realized Mr. Taggert wasn't amused (no big surprise there), so he said, "I'm building a castle for the kids. If it works out, I can give you the plans and you can make one for B. J."

"A castle?"

"Yeah."

Mr. Taggert frowned, then walked away mumbling.

Mrs. Gilford, our principal, did the same thing when she came out onto the playground and saw Dad pasting up fake advertisements on the front walls of the stores and the hotel he built on our playground. She didn't see a need for such detail on toys that would wear down anyway. Dad told her the kids would make their own advertisements when his wore out. They did, too. Every fifth-grade class made advertisements for their history class and pasted them up.

Dad had to be the greatest, messiest, strangest, most dangerous, and least understood dad around. And I felt like I was an itch and a prayer away from losing him, and no one knew what to do.

Sitting in Mom's workshop, eating ice cream and staring

at the limp hammock out the window, I realized how empty a room could feel even when it was filled with almost a literal ton of rock. The hammock started to swing in the breeze. I smiled at the thought of how much Dad loved napping out there. That image grew into an idea in a flash.

"Mom," I said, turning to her as she cleaned her tools. "Why don't we bring Dad here?"

Dragging Dad's spirit to the hospital didn't work, so bringing Dad's body to the house had to be the next best step to getting the two dads back together.

"Then he wouldn't have so far to travel to get home?" Mom tried not to laugh.

"You said he was taking a risk every time he came home, because it brought him away from his body. So, let's bring him all home."

Mom thought on it a moment, tapping a chisel on her workbench. "The hospital isn't doing anything for him we can't do with a hired nurse keeping an eye on all of us."

"Can we try it?" I jumped off my stool.

Mom nodded. "Indeed. He belongs at home anyway." I could have hugged Mom until she grew old.

Unfortunately, the idea turned out to be a lot harder to put into action than it was to think up. Dr. Parker didn't like the risk of Dad being away from the hospital, where they could help him breathe if they needed to or avert all kinds of possible medical disasters.

Mom talked about familiar sounds and smells, the

comforts of home that might help Dad heal faster. Dr. Parker nodded, but I could tell by the not-a-good-idea look in her eye that Mom hadn't convinced her yet. Mom suggested hiring emergency medical technicians (the EMT folks who come to your rescue when you dial 911) to be there all day, every day. Those people had the training to help Dad in an emergency.

Dr. Parker chewed her pen over that idea, then said, "If you do that, I could sign the release forms."

And with that Dad came home—hospital bed, monitors, IV tree, liquid food, EMT, and all. We converted our study room into a sleeping room, and the place looked like a hospital in no time. That night we all sat around Dad's bed. Practicing our southern accents, we read to him in turn from *To Kill a Mockingbird* (Dad loved Boo Radley) while Gary Larkin, the EMT, played solitaire in the hall.

An Into-Body
Experience

I dreamed of Dad sitting up in bed asking for pickles dipped in ice cream, but he didn't. He slept without snoring. His eyes did twitter a bit, but the daytime EMT, Carol Kempf, said his nerves sometimes went on automatic pilot and did things like that.

All day I waited for Dad's spirit to show up so we could try again, but the hours passed and nothing happened— the monitors blipped, the IV dripped, and Dad didn't move in the real world or otherwise. I talked to him. Mom sang. Samuel told him stupid jokes. Joliet walked the house searching for a sign of his spirit self.

Evening came and Mom forced me to go to piano practice. Truth be told, I had to do something—anything—to quiet the electrified feeling that pulsed through my body when I thought about Dad. His body still slept on, but where had his spirit gone?

At piano practice Mr. Lynch went on and on about the healing power of music. I pressed down real hard, hoping a string would snap so I wouldn't have to play anymore.

"Yes. Good, Mr. Jones," he said, nodding in time.

I pounded my way through Beethoven's "Für Elise" for

the fourth time. I just wanted to go home and see if Dad had shown up again.

As I finished, Mr. Lynch patted my hands, saying, "That should be enough for today. I think even Beethoven could've heard your playing."

I didn't bother to say good-bye. I just went outside to wait for Mom to pick me up.

Sitting on the steps, I heard Dad's voice say, "*Countertenor.*"

"What?" I asked, spinning to the side. There he sat in his dumpy old housecoat. I needed to hug him so bad my chest hurt.

"*A guy who can sing higher than a tenor is called a countertenor. I don't know why I've been thinking about that lately. It's like someone dropped it in my ear when I wasn't looking.*"

Even if he couldn't answer us, part of Dad had heard B. J. and me that night. "I'm so glad to see you, Dad."

"*Likewise.*"

"Where'd you go? Do you remember anything?"

Dad shook his head.

"I'm sorry about the hospital."

"*It's pretty tough standing outside your own body watching yourself gasp for air—like being trapped in an episode of* The Twilight Zone."

"Well, I've got a new plan."

"*Really?*" I'm not sure if Dad's image faded a little or he actually shivered at the idea.

"It's a good one, Dad. This time we brought your body to you."

"Excuse me?"

"Your body's at home. We moved it there."

"You make me sound like a used car that quit running. You just towed it on home." Dad trailed his hand in the air to imitate a traveling tow truck.

"It might work."

"It could indeed, Ebon." He patted me on the knee, and I felt the tiniest bit of pressure.

"Hey, I felt that."

"You did? I've been practicing." Dad had just raised his hand to try again when Mom rolled up in the Jeep.

"Hop in," I said to Dad as I opened the door.

"Hey, Ebon. How was practice?" Mom called.

Dad crawled into the backseat. *"Anything's better than traveling by bus."*

"Is Dad with you?" Mom asked, turning toward Dad. "Luke?"

"Howdy, sweet." Dad leaned forward and tried to kiss Mom. At the last second I put my hand on Mom's leg, hoping it'd help.

"Oh." Mom brushed her check. "What was that? It felt like an electrical shock."

Dad looked up, saying, *"Thank you, God."*

"Dad," I told Mom. "He can almost touch people now."

Whirling around, Mom said, "Luke, don't mess with this. If

you keep pushing yourself, you're liable to lose the body God gave you, and He doesn't go around handing out seconds."

"It's okay, Wynne. I'll be careful."

"Thank you," Mom said, facing the road. I could tell she felt like crying. She bit her lip and blinked real hard. We rode home in silence.

Mom and I held hands as we led the way into the house. Joliet sat by Dad's bed basting together pieces of a quilt. Dad stood in the doorway staring as if he'd found a dead body in the room instead of a sleeping one.

"It's okay, Luke." Mom stood next to him.

"Dad?" Joliet whirled out of her chair. Grabbing me, she smiled. "Good to see you, Daddy!"

"You, too, Jolie Bear." He reached up to touch her but closed his hand as he saw Mom's eyes narrow.

I heard someone fiddling around in the kitchen. When Samuel came running down the stairs, I knew it had to be the EMT.

"Did I hear Dad?" Samuel asked. He walked right up to me and put his hand on my shoulder, as if to plug himself in. I'd begun to feel like a human battery.

"Hi, Dad. Like your new digs?"

Dad shuddered, but forced a smile. *"Sure thing."*

"Let's give it a try, Luke," Mom suggested.

"What about Gary?" Joliet nodded toward the kitchen.

"Right." Mom put up her finger in recognition. "Gary?" she called.

"Yeah?"

"I . . . think we should . . . have candles in here . . . in case of a power outage." Mom shrugged as she fumbled to think of a way to get rid of him for a while. We all nodded to urge her to keep going. She had a great start.

"Good idea." Gary came out of the kitchen eating a sandwich. "All of my equipment runs on batteries, but the more light we've got, the better."

"Then would you mind bringing some down for me?" Mom put her arms around us kids. "I'd really like to spend some time with Luke and the kids."

Gary nodded. "Sure. Where are they?"

"In the cabinets in the kitchenette on the fourth floor."

"All righty." Gary headed upstairs. The cabinets in my room were so full of stuff you'd think a family of seven lived up there. He'd be hunting for a good long time.

"Okay," Dad rubbed his hands together, but it barely made a whispering sound. *"Let's do this."*

He stepped forward, but Mom stopped him by saying, "Wait. We should try together." Mom gave me a nudge. "We'll all hold on to each other."

Scrambling around, we linked hands. Joliet and Mom leaned over the bed to complete the circle as Dad watched from the doorway. Feeling almost like we'd started our own séance so Dad could have an into-body experience, I squeezed Dad's real hand hard.

"Ah!" Dad's spirit raised his hand in pain.

"Sorry, Dad."

I laughed with a thrill of excitement as Joliet said, "This might work."

"All right, Luke," Mom said. "It's your turn."

Dad walked forward. Samuel's hand shook in mine. When Dad passed through Mom, she let out a sigh of shock like she did when she stepped into cold water. He went right into the bed, but not into himself. Nothing blocked his path as he came toward me. In a rush that made me dizzy, Samuel's hand fell out of mine. I heard the tune to some weird Irish song, which made my foot tap. I saw flashes of water, felt mist on my face, then I appeared over Mom as she weeded the garden. I thought for a moment that I was standing on a ladder—she looked so far away. But no, I saw her as Dad did, from more than six feet up. I looked at Mom through Dad's eyes. Felt what he did. Heard his memories. Before I could wrap my mind around this whole weird event, a wave of sadness crashed into a state of panic. I cried out. Then just as quick, I felt tired and jittery, even empty.

"What happened?" Mom let go of Joliet and Dad, then came around the bed to me.

Dad's spirit appeared on the other side. *"You okay, Eb?"*

I mumbled and stumbled and shook my way through a description of what'd happened. Mom nodded, trying to stay calm. Dad backed up.

"Dad?" I asked, hoping he'd tell me why he looked like I'd said I'd seen my own ghost.

"*You heard my thoughts, felt my feelings.*" Turning to Mom, he asked, "*Did you, Wynne?*"

Mom shook her head. "No. Just felt a twinge like a sudden shiver."

Dad looked at me. "*But you felt me?*" Dad tapped his chest. "*Inside me.*"

"I guess so."

Dad kept backing up. "*I don't like this. God can send me to purgatory, for all I care, but you kids have to stay safe. This is going too far.*"

He walked right through the couch in the grown-up lounge and disappeared. *What now?* I thought. My solutions all seemed to push Dad farther away, but to where?

A Helping
Hand

The whole fouled-up back-into-body experience had everyone edgy. Even Samuel acted like he'd downed a whole pot of coffee—twitchy, angry, and impossible to please. We all had to go to our separate parts of the house to keep from launching into stupid fights about anything but what was really upsetting us—Dad. The tension made me jumpy. Like a cougar in a cage, I kept walking back and forth on the second-floor landing. As I passed Joliet's room for the thousandth time I noticed she had immersed herself in an art project. I went in to see what she was up to.

She had a big, flat board with all sorts of curvy rivers cut into the wood. She'd painted here and there in blues and greens, kind of mixing them together so they looked like clouds would if they stuck around during a tornado.

While I was watching, she picked out photographs, then cut out images of Dad and the rest of us to piece together along the rivers. She cut smooth, wavy edges so she could fit a picture of Dad at a barbecue next to a picture of Samuel and me giving each other the death grip of love (that's a happy headlock). With each picture of Dad, Joliet cut out pictures of the rest of us to fit around him. Dad was with us all over the board.

"I miss him too," I told her.

"This will be all we have when he's gone."

"He's not going to die."

Joliet put her scissors down to say, "Why else would he be a ghost? He's just being stubborn as usual. He won't hold out forever."

Her words flipped me around inside like I was on a slow-moving roller coaster that still took the wind out of me. What if she was right? I heard Grandma Helen say, "Knowing Luke Jones, he'd find a way to go home, dead or not." Dad was fighting against the nature of things, as usual. But how?

There's a logic to most things—electricity, the number system, grocery stores—but what's the logic of ghosts? Mom had her own logic about Dad's situation. Joliet had hers. I had mine, but who was right? Would Dad go back into his body and wake up? Was Dad fighting to stay out of heaven?

I wanted to say something to make Joliet feel better, but as I watched her put picture pieces together I figured she was doing well enough on her own.

I slid off the bed and went down the back stairs. On my way down I heard the growl of one of Mom's sanders. She had slipped into gargoyle-spawning mode. When I walked into her workshop, I saw Mom's head poking out of a jungle of potted rose bushes covered with protective plastic. Hanging over the edge of a stool like a human gargoyle,

Mom wore her welding helmet as she ground away on a gray rock the size of a gallon jug of orange juice. The vague outlines of a human face stared out at me.

I just stood in the doorway and watched the rock dust fly. Mom used these handheld grinders that were kind of like those ear-ringing buzzy things dentists used to grind your teeth down to put a filling in. Those drill things made it feel like there was a mini jackhammer going at it in my mouth. Samuel and I have always called those gadgets teeth chewers. Mom's tools were like industrial-strength teeth chewers, so we called them rock chewers.

To make a gargoyle, she'd get a big hunk of rock, then she'd take a hammer and a chisel and hack away until it looked like a ridgy, flat-sided desert mountain, or the big chunks of chocolate in the DQ commercials. After that she'd take out the rock chewers and grind away. They were loud enough to be heard from the Shroom Forest when she didn't close her studio door.

Zippo, they turned stone to dust. The rock started out all jagged and rock looking, then whir, grind, grizzle—puffs of dust clouded over the rock. Mom stood up and backed away. The dust cleared, and zammo! There was a smooth, rounded, living-looking thing, especially when she used her mini rock chewer and nibbled away to create the eyes. I don't know why, but eyes always made the gargoyles come alive. When they could look back at me, I knew there was life there.

Mom didn't set out to make a certain kind of monster, she just let her creative juices charge up and lead the way through the rock. One time she even made a cow gargoyle. It was so funny looking we put it on a shelf over the kitchen sink.

This rock revealed itself in slow motion. Mom paused as she worked, waiting for something to tell her what to do next. I'd seen her work before, but it seemed like I *had* to stay and watch this time. I got another stool and kept my eyes on that rock. Each time the dust settled, I got a look at the beast taking shape. Mom made a faint curve, then she stuck her rock chewer into the curve like she was drilling a hole in a board. Little by little she made spikes. Switching to a real tiny chewer, she finished off the spikes until they looked like blades of grass. From there she moved down to carve out a wrinkled forehead. Skipping over the eyes, she made ears that were curvy but human. I saw what was coming as she shaped the chin—Dad. Mom was sculpting Dad out of rock.

She finished out the lips with the deep dip above them and started in on the nose; she worked faster, as if she were racing someone else. I lost her in the rock dust for a while, and I daydreamed of Dad's face, comparing the rock I'd seen to him. When the dust settled, Dad stared at us both, his lips wide in a smile, his hair pointing to the sky, his eyes happy to see us.

Mom's helmet was caked with rock dust. When she

flipped up the shield on her helmet, I could see she'd been crying. "I miss him so much."

"Me, too."

Mom ran her fingers over the rock face. I could see by the look in her eyes that she wished it were really Dad she was touching, like she did when she helped him shave on Sunday mornings before church. He was always too slow.

"He's going to wake up, Ebon."

What if it never happens? I didn't even want to hear the thought, but it was possible. Dad could sleep forever. What would I do?

B. J. didn't talk for a week when her grandpa Roger died. I was only two when Grandpa Winslow died, so I didn't know what I'd do. I didn't want to know.

Mom stood up. "Let's go get some fresh air."

I followed her out onto the lawn. It was almost dark (gargoyles were no quick business). The Taggerts sat at the picnic table in their backyard drinking tea. It was just Mr. Taggert and Rita. B. J. was probably at ceramics class with Grandma Helen. The Taggerts laughed as Mom and I came up to take a seat at the picnic table.

"Hello, Wynne, Ebon." Rita held up her glass to us. "We were just remembering the time Luke made that ginger-bread house."

Mr. Taggert howled with laughter. Mom shook her head as Rita kept right on going, "There was frosting all over the kitchen, you had burned gingerbread everywhere."

"And it just fell apart," Mr. Taggert added.

Dad did a lot of funny stuff, but the collapse of the gingerbread house wasn't his fault, anyway. Uncle Todd had accidentally hooked up the coffeepot right behind it, and the heat from the coffeepot melted the frosting that held the house together.

Mom said, "I loved it when he built the igloo by the pond in the park."

"Didn't Ebon fall in the water that night?" Mr. Taggert asked.

I did. I lost my footing on the slick shore and I slid right in. The pond's more of a big pit than a body of water, so I was in over my head when I went under, flailing away in my snowsuit. I couldn't even swim in all that fabric. Dad came in after me. At his height he could touch bottom and push me back to shore. We spent the night shivering next to the fireplace, Mom bringing us hot chocolate. I could taste the hint of mint in the hot chocolate from the candy-cane stir stick Mom always put in.

"Jumping in that water would've probably given me a heart attack." Mr. Taggert shivered.

We all sat in silence for a minute, then Rita leaned back, saying, "I remember how he sang 'If I Had a Hammer' for three hours straight when he fixed our roof after Albert here fell off the ladder and hurt his knee."

Mr. Taggert rubbed his knee. "Oh, don't remind me."

They all laughed. Mom launched into the story about

Dad putting Mom's spitting gargoyles onto the ends of the gutters on the roof, but the stories just made me long for Dad, so I left.

I headed for the climbing tree in the park behind our house. A year before, Mom'd set up the camera on this big tripod she rented, and we all climbed into that huge, old maple tree for a family picture. It looked great, with Samuel wedged in a crook of the tree. Joliet dangled over a branch, and Mom pretended to feed her leaves. Dad and I leaned against either side of the trunk, holding a branch of leaves between us. I loved that picture. When we took it, I thought it'd be great to take a family photo there every year, but Dad's coma changed all that.

Scaling the tree, I plopped down on a branch. I could see a Frisbee on the ground below. Scooching farther out, I got right above it and started to throw twirly-copter maple seeds down at it. I ran out of ammo, so I leaned forward to get some more, but the nearest cluster hung just out of reach. Stretching until I felt a little swirl in my stomach, I teetered, tried to correct myself, then slipped right off the branch. It was weird, but I felt kind of weightless as I plummeted face first to the ground.

Grabbing for branches, I clutched at twigs that snapped, crashed through a thin branch, then jolted to a stop. Had I hit the ground? I didn't feel any pain. No, something had caught me around the neck. As I got yanked onto a sturdy branch I saw Dad, his legs anchored around the trunk, his face stretched under the strain of pulling me up by the back of my shirt.

"Dad!" I screamed, amazed that he had really touched me.

"You all right?"

"You touched me!" I reached out, but my hand went right through his shoulder.

He grabbed his shoulder. *"Ouch."*

"It hurt?"

"A little. Maybe I pulled a muscle catching you."

I shook my head in amazement. As Dad rubbed his shoulder I thought back to the car ride home. "What if Mom was wrong about you having only one body? Could you really will your way into a new one?"

Dad laughed. *"Ebon, I know I've got a mind of my own, but I don't think I've got that kind of brain power."*

"Oh."

Dad patted his chest. *"My heart's beating time with a Dixie jazz band. You sure you're okay?"*

"I'm fine. How'd you just show up like that?"

He looked at me and smiled, saying, *"I was in that weird library I told you about, then all of the sudden I heard you yelling, and whallube! I materialized right above you as you fell. I just grabbed, praying my hand would hold."*

"Dad, how come you never show up where Samuel or Joliet is? Not even Mom. It's like we're twins who can't be apart. Where I go, you go."

Dad raised his eyebrows as if to say something about us

being twins, but then he sighed, saying, *"Poor Wynne. I saw her working back there."* He pointed over his shoulder.

"The gargoyle?"

"It's like watching bees creating a hive." The distant look in Dad's eyes said he was watching Mom craft the gargoyle all over again in his mind's eye.

"But Dad, why's it always me? No one can even see you if they're not touching me."

Dad shrugged. *"Why do only some people see ghosts? And how come there are folks who see twenty-twenty while some are born blind?"* Dad patted his knee. *"We all see a little differently. You, my junior Ghostbuster, can see a little further into most things."*

"How come I can't see where you go? Maybe if I did, I could lead you back to your body."

"Curious idea, but wherever I go, it's not a place for healthy kids."

I fell quiet for a while. I knew what I wanted to say, but I was afraid of saying it. Finally I opened my mouth, but nothing came out.

"What if I died?" Dad whispered it.

"Yeah."

"Then I'd go off for good and wait for the rest of you to show up in your own time."

"It's not funny, Dad."

"I wasn't making a joke, Ebon. Everyone dies." He made dying sound as normal as sneezing.

"Why?"

"*Because the earth is crowded enough without having every-body who was ever born still on it. Although I'd like to sit down with Paul or Peter and find out what Jesus was really like as a living, breathing person.*"

"Dad."

"*What?*"

I shook my head. He was impossible sometimes. I asked, "But why would you go into a coma and die?"

"*If you're asking for a medical explanation, you're asking the wrong quack. My doctorate's in history. If you're looking for a way-of-the-world-type explanation, I'm really unqualified to answer.*"

"You have a guess for everything, Dad."

He looked down at the ground, then said, "*Then I guess it happened by accident. I reached out for a hammer, lost my balance, and fell off a ladder. It was that simple, like getting lost. Now I just have to find my way home.*"

"Ebon!" Joliet screamed as if she were being torn in half.

"*Jolie!*" Dad jumped from the tree, but he never reached the ground; he just disappeared.

"Ebon!" Joliet howled again.

I scampered down the tree, yelling, "What is it?"

Joliet stopped running, then started back toward the house, shouting, "It's Dad! Alarms started going off!"

A Final
Solution

No. It can't be happening, I thought as we ran for the house.
Dad's going to be okay. He'd touched me. I could almost feel
his fingers scrape across my back as he grabbed my shirt.

The house seemed to be a marathon away as we ran. I
couldn't help wondering if Mom had been right after all.
Did Dad risk losing his body by making his spirit turn
solid? Or was Dad pulling himself back together in reverse?
Bringing his physical body into his spirit, one part at a
time.

Mom met us in the backyard, yelling, "It's okay, kids.
False alarm."

"False alarm?" Joliet asked, shocked. "Every bell and
whistle in the house was going off when I left."

Mom gave Joliet a hug and rubbed her arms to calm her
down. "He's going to be fine." She reached out to take me
in as she said, "Gary said sometimes a surge in electricity
can set them off."

"So nothing happened?" I asked Mom as we came in
through the back door.

"Either that or your dad went into full cardiac arrest
then back to normal all by himself." Mom said it like it was
a joke, but the thought made me shiver. Dad could have

risked his life by saving me. Maybe he was pulling too hard to make his spirit whole. I had to do something soon.

Walking up to Dad's bed, I realized just how much thinner he'd gotten since he'd fallen asleep. It looked like only skin lined the bones in his face. Afraid to touch him, I couldn't move. I heard Mom assuring Samuel by telling him Dad had probably slipped right into a dream about flying zebra-striped hippos or something of the like. Samuel giggled.

I reached out to touch Dad's arm as Mom walked up to take his other hand. I could see the shape of his arm under the sheet. I grabbed for his fingers, but my hand never found them. Passing through a cloud of static, my hand sank right to the bed. I pulled my hand back.

Dad had started to dissolve!

Mom held his other hand. Part of him was still solid. What could I do? My mind spun. I reached back into the cloud of static, hoping to find something within. Dad's thoughts perhaps, just like the time when he passed through me and our minds linked up like mental Siamese twins.

At first I felt only a biting warmth, like the zap of electricity when you rub two staticky socks together, then the feeling deepened, traveling to my heart. Dad's thoughts drifted in like a dream. *Hold on. Hold on. Hold on.*

"Hold on to what, Dad?"

"Can you hear him, Ebon?" Mom looked at me.

I yanked my hand back, saying, "No."

I lied because I knew Mom wouldn't like my plan for finding Dad any more than he favored the idea of me following him. I wished I'd jumped out of that tree after him. I might've slid right into the place he went to when he wasn't with us. We could walk back together.

Or you could be stuck here like me, Dad whispered.

The thought gave me the chills, but I couldn't let it stop me. I waited, knowing I could try again when everyone went to sleep. Gary did his paperwork in the kitchen around eleven; I could try then.

We all sat with Dad until well past dark, then Mom said we should get some sleep.

"Let's camp out here with Dad," Samuel suggested. "We could all bring down our sleeping bags."

Protesting would have clued everyone in, so I agreed to Samuel's plan along with Mom and Joliet. I even dozed off for a bit, but when I woke up, the house had gone quiet. Gary was reading a book in the hallway.

I got up without making anyone else stir. Climbing into the bed next to Dad, wedged against the metal rail, I lay down and put my arm where his arm should've been. My skin tingled as if my arm had fallen asleep. Moving sent little prickles of heat up my arm.

I started drifting downward as memories fell around me like leaves—a boy jumping into a creek; Joliet outfitting Tinkerbell for the play; a cotton-candy machine in full spin; a baby Samuel eating chocolate cake with his hands; Mom hanging a birdhouse in the backyard; me playing with Fred at the keys of the piano.

Ebon? Dad's voice echoed in my head.

"Dad?" I called back, slipping past a shelf of books. Settling on uncertain ground, I stood before the shelf, dizzy and a little giggly.

"*Ebon, what are you doing here?*" Dad came toward me from down an aisle of books. He shimmered like a car approaching through waves of heat rising off a highway.

I'd found him. Now what?

"*Dad.*" I held my hands out.

"*We have to get you home.*" Dad stood behind me, nudging me forward as if he felt afraid to touch me.

Taking his hands, I pulled his arms around me, saying, "*Let's go together.*"

We took a left turn, then a right. For a moment I thought we'd turned around. A maze sprawled out around us. Dad held me closer as a phone began ringing in the distance.

"*It's Mom, Dad. She's looking for us.*" I felt her like I did when I read her letters at camp. Her written words brought her to me—or at least her love, anyway.

Phones rang all around us as we turned and walked, then turned again.

"*They're looking, Dad. Everyone—Samuel, Joliet, even B. J.'s there.*"

Dad stopped. "*Let's stand still and listen.*"

Silence, then a distant voice like someone whispering in the next room. "And when she woke up, a woman showed up on her wall, all dressed in red, sitting in a sleigh, a bearded man standing next to her." Samuel telling a ghost story.

"Do you hear it?"

"I hear it." Dad's breath warmed my ear.

"Ebon wouldn't tell me how Attila the Hun died, so I asked my Aunt Betty, she's a high school history teacher," B. J. said from just a ways ahead. "She says Attila the Hun had too much to drink on his wedding night and choked on his own vomit. I could have gone a long time without knowing that. And it's all your fault that I know it now, Luke Jones. You tell your son the most disgusting things. Disgusting."

Dad and I laughed. It echoed as if we stood in a gymnasium, bouncing like a basketball thrown hard against the floor.

"Should I wake Ebon up for dinner, Mom?" Joliet's voice echoed off the shelves.

"No, let him sleep. The poor kid probably hasn't slept through the night in a week."

We drifted down an aisle of books; they slowly shifted into blackness as if they'd been covered by a blanket.

Joliet's voice bounded back in, like she was speaking right in our ears. "Did you hear me, you guys? I said, the Tinsdale triplets want me to make them a costume so they can go to the party as three peas in a pod."

We drifted past the voices to a door made of complex pieces of wood, each one carved to show a part of our life—Joliet's sewing machine slipped in as the nose of Mom's farmer gargoyle; the hand of Samuel's fire-fighting ghost pushed my skateboard.

"*No handle,*" Dad said, pressing a few pieces.

"*We've got to solve it,*" I told him.

Scanning the puzzle, Dad asked, "*Where are we?*"

I could see things, but no people. Then I recognized the elephant hair pin Joliet used to prevent her from sewing any of her long hair into the hem of a costume. Sure enough, the puzzle piece showed the pin stuck in a hive of Joliet's hair. Mom's eyes looked down at me from the top of a bowl of her ring salad. "*We're all here, Dad. In pieces.*" I tapped Joliet's hair bun.

"*A-ha!*"

Dad and I set to work, pushing our family together piece by piece—an eye, an ear, a left arm. Our tree family picture formed in a sea of the things that filled our life. As I slid the piece of my right shoulder against one side of the tree trunk, Dad pushed his left-shoulder piece up to the other side, and our real fingers touched.

A chill of excitement sped through my body, and I linked into Dad's memories: standing in the theater doorway watching me play in my recital last spring, and how it made him nearly shake with pride; him checking my homework after everyone had gone to bed, laughing with pleasure at how I'd taken bits and pieces from our history talks and planted them in my papers, nodding when I made a point he'd never thought of himself; me traveling with him to the library, where he stopped at the reference desk to visit with Mr. Heflig to share stories about his kids—how Juliet could shoot an apple off a horse's rump, the way Samuel recited the periodic table of elements like a poem, and the fact that I could remember everything he ever told me. But Dad had never told me about all these things. And when that instant flash ended, the door swung open and I felt like I could fly.

Home Again, Whole Again

Staring into the dining room of Hamilton Hall, I promised myself that before the end of Christmas break Dad would be able to tell Mr. Heflig story after story about the millions of the things we'd done together. As Dad stepped into the room, passing under a ladder, I could feel myself settling back to Earth, noticing the weight of my own body, smelling the dust, hearing my pulse echoing in my ears.

"Back to the beginning." Dad slapped a rung.

"Are we really here?" I spun around; gum wrappers and sand crunched beneath my feet. We never even cleaned the place after the crowds walked through.

Dad ran his fingers over his cheeks. "I feel real," he said, his voice hiking up a notch. Grabbing me around the waist, he spun me in a circle, shouting, "You feel real!"

I hugged him, breathing in his smell of pickle juice and sweat, squeezing him to feel his muscles and know he wouldn't disappear in my hand. Laughter bubbled out of me as he set me down. I asked, "But are we here? Really here?"

Dad pulled a tapestry off the wall to reveal a window. The moonlight streaming in startled me for a second.

"I see home," he said.

"Last one there washes the dishes!" I scrambled for the window. Yanking it open, I nearly fell out. Dad climbed right over me. He scooped me up and made for the backyard.

Stopping in front of Castle Rook, Dad looked at the house. All the windows looked gray in the moonlight. Dad whispered, "One A.M. and all's quiet."

I started to cry and hugged him so hard my arms nearly went numb.

Bouncing me in the air, Dad shouted, "No tears, Sir Harout! We've got an army to raise!" Dad set me on my feet, then raced toward the Styrofoam cannons he'd rigged up on the roof of the turret. "Come on!"

Laughing, I ran for the cannon by the front gate. As I loaded mine with leaves Dad said, "I wish we had water balloons!"

"Me, too," I shouted through happy tears.

Sending off a volley, we pelted the house, bringing everyone to the windows overlooking the backyard.

"Ho-ho!" Dad shouted when he saw Mom stick her head out. "Look who's home!"

"Dad!" Joliet leaned way out of her sewing-annex window. I thought she was going to jump.

Samuel came tearing out the back door as Mom said, "I'm coming!"

Dad grabbed Samuel under the shoulders and swung him around in a circle. "Sir Obb, the flying knight."

"Hug me, Daddy. Hug me!"

Dad obliged and threw in a mess of kisses to boot. As I ran up to them Joliet came charging out the back door and joined in. Hugging and kissing and crying, she tried to talk but couldn't.

Mom stepped outside but didn't come to us. She just stood there like she expected us to run off. "Tell me it's true." Her cheeks quivered as if she was trying not to smile. "Tell me I can see four solid people standing in our backyard."

Dad held Joliet's and Samuel's hands in one of his own and mine in the other. He raised all our hands, shouting, "The knights of Castle Rook salute you, dear lady!"

"Yes!" Mom flew into the air. When she came down, we all hugged. We laughed. We kissed. We cried. We pinched. We squealed. We even stomped on one another's feet, just to be sure.

Just then, we heard a scream from inside the house.

"Gary." Mom looked spooked.

Gary came stumbling out of the house looking as if he'd taken a ride inside a dryer. "I fell asleep. Mr. Jones is gone. The bed's empty. The monitor's dead. It shorted out."

Seeing Dad, he flew into a panic, insisting that we take Dad straight to the hospital. The hospital staff got bent out of shape over what Dad labeled a reverse séance. Little did they know how far we'd really gone to wake him up. In the walk back to our world Dad and I must have dragged our physical bodies right along with us.

A
Miracle

The doctors said Dad could be classified as a modern medical miracle, the way he just woke up. We spent more time at the hospital in the next few weeks than at home. Tests showed he could stand to gain a few pounds, and it took quite some time before he could even climb the front steps without getting winded. The coma had knocked all the strength right out of him, but not one other hint of his extended nap showed up on any of the tests they ran. All signs of an injury to Dad's brain had vanished—that old rip just disappeared. Dr. Ventro kept calling to see how we were readjusting, but we just let him babble into the answering machine.

The whole Jones family Rip van Winkle adventure could be classified as a miracle in my book. For the first time, when Dad had gone into hiding, I'd found him. Now I was Ebon Jones, the boy who went beyond this world and halfway through the next to bring his dad home. It wasn't a skill I planned to use often, but I wasn't complaining.

Neither was anyone else in the family. Joliet had already started on a Siamese twins costume for Dad and me to wear next Halloween. Samuel practiced the new tale he had to tell—one nobody had ever heard before, the story of the ghost of a living person. And this one he knew to be true. Mom carved a statue of Dad and me making our way back, surrounded by books and listening for the voices of home. She placed it on Dad's desk, right next to his computer. But for a long time after his big sleep, I didn't see Dad even go into his office.

After the doctors finally gave us the green light, Mom and Dad decided a family vacation was in order. They wrote notes to our teachers, and we spent the week curled up in the Shroom Forest with a new book, roving around Castle Rook and its grounds, having picnics on the glade, and simply lounging around.

When the week ended, I figured we'd all swing back into our normal routine. I walked downstairs the following Monday morning expecting to fling kookleberries at Samuel, but Dad stood at the stove flipping pancakes. Not only was he up, he'd combed his hair, shaved, and gotten dressed.

"Dad, it's seven thirty."

"Plenty of time for chocolate chip pancakes with hot fudge, whipped cream, and a cherry on top," Dad said, bringing a stack of steaming pancakes to the table.

"Yeah!" Samuel shouted from his seat.

"What comes after the dessert?" Joliet laughed.

"An apple." Dad smiled. "But we can eat those on the way to school."

"You're driving us?" I asked.

"Yep." Dad went to the microwave to get the hot fudge he'd heated up.

I turned to look around for Mom. "Is Mom sick?"

"Healthy as a newborn baby."

Mom came in with a grocery bag. "Got the milk," she said, holding up the bag.

"Pour it on," Dad shouted.

"I'll take mine in a glass," Joliet joked.

Sitting down, I figured Dad's need to be around us all of the time hadn't worn off yet.

"You're putting on *A Christmas Carol* at school, right?" Dad looked at each of us to show he wanted everyone to answer.

I stared at Dad as he listened to Samuel recite all of his lines from his role as the Ghost of Christmas Yet to Come. Dad actually listened and smiled and nodded. "You think they could use some help building the sets?" He took a big bite and gave himself a whipped-cream mustache.

"I know I could use some help," Joliet said. "I have over fifty costumes to sew and only one assistant."

"I could be in charge of buttons," Dad offered.

We laughed. Dad couldn't sew in a straight line if he tried to put a border on a ruler.

"What about you, Ebon?"

"Ebenezer Scrooge," I whispered. With a name like Ebon, I'd gotten plenty of Scrooge jokes. In fact, most of the kids figured they'd played a great joke on me by giving me the role. But I'd be the one laughing when my performance turned out to be a ticket to future roles.

"Way to go." Dad gave me a shake. "I'll be there. Front row."

And he was.

With all the time Dad spent cutting out patterns with Joliet, reciting lines with me and Samuel, and polishing gargoyles for Mom, I knew he'd really spoken from his heart when he said he'd settle into a new routine. Nothing could make my dad ordinary, but the whole Rip van Winkle ordeal had shown him how to be around when we needed him.

He didn't exactly reinvent himself. He just stuck to normal hours, like any other working dad. He started his research at nine and shut off the computer at five. Of course, he snuck in for a quick romp around the Internet when he couldn't sleep. But everybody works overtime, right? Now if only we could get him to stop eating cucumbers before he goes to bed.